Barbara Cartland, the v
who is also an historian, p
television personality, h
over 390 million books o

She has also had many historical works published and has
written four autobiographies as well as the biographies of her
mother and that of her brother, Ronald Cartland, who was the
first Member of Parliament to be killed in the last war. This book
has a preface by Sir Winston Churchill and has just been repub-
lished with an introduction by Sir Arthur Bryant. *Love at the
Helm*, a novel written with the help and inspiration of the late Earl
Mountbatten of Burma, Uncle of His Royal Highness Prince
Philip, is being sold for the Mountbatten Memorial Trust. Miss
Cartland in 1978 sang an Album of Love Songs with the Royal
Philharmonic Orchestra.

In 1976 by writing twenty-one books, she broke the world
record and has continued for the following eight years with 24, 20,
23, 24, 24, 25, 22, 26. In *The Guinness Book of Records* she is listed
as the world's top-selling author.

In private life Barbara Cartland, who is a Dame of Grace of the
Order of St. John of Jerusalem, Chairman of the St. John Council
in Hertfordshire and Deputy President of the St. John Ambulance
Brigade, has fought for better conditions and salaries for Midwives and Nurses.

She has championed the cause for old people, had the law
altered regarding gypsies and founded the first Romany Gypsy
camp in the world.

Barbara Cartland is deeply interested in Vitamin therapy and is
President of the National Association for Health.

Her designs "Decorating with Love" are being sold all over the
U.S.A. and the National Home Fashions League made her, in
1981, "Woman of Achievement".

Barbara Cartland's Romances (Book of Cartoons) has been
published in Great Britain, and the U.S.A.

Barbara Cartland's book *Getting Older, Growing Younger,* and
her cookery book *The Romance of Food* have been published in
Great Britain, the U.S.A., and in other parts of the world. She has
also written a Children's Pop-Up Book entitled *Princess to the
Rescue.*

In 1984 she received at Kennedy Airport America's Bishop
Wright Air Industry Award for her contribution to the development of aviation when, in 1931, she and two R.A.F. officers
thought of, and carried, the first aeroplane-towed glider Air-Mail.

BARBARA CARTLAND

AN ANGEL RUNS AWAY

Pan Original
Pan Books London and Sydney

First published 1986 by Pan Books Ltd.
Cavaye Place, London SW10 9PG
9 8 7 6 5 4 3 2 1
© Cartland Promotions 1985
ISBN 0 330 29544 6
Printed and bound in Great Britain by
Hunt Barnard Printing, Aylesbury, Bucks

BARBARA CARTLAND'S EXPERIENCE ON HEALTH

1930-1932 Studied Herbal Medicine with the famous Mrs Leyel of Culpeper.

1931-1933 A patient and a student of Dr Dengler of Baden-Baden. First use of olive oil as an internal treatment of liver complaints, colitis and inflammation of the bowel.

1930-1937 Helped Lady Rhys Williams giving Vitamin B for habitual abortion and malnutrition in the Distressed Areas.

Studied the first use of Vitamin E with brood mares and later for barren women.

1935 onwards Worked with Dr Pierre Lansel, M.D. first Practioner in England to give injections of Vitamins B and C. Followed his experiments with hormones for rejuvenation and the Nieheims treatment of Cell Therapy. Studied with two eminent Doctors the effect of oil injection on external haemorrhoids.

Studied the nutritional conditions in her brother's Parliamentary Constituency, King's Norton Division of Birmingham, where there was malnutrition from unemployment.

Practised Yoga exercises and breathing with the only white Yogi in the world. Wrote in a monthly magazine on the subject.

Studied nutrition in Montreal and did two lecture tours in lower Canada during which visited a large number of schools and hospitals.

1919-1945 County Cadet Officer for the St. John Ambulance Brigade, Bedfordshire. Arranged First Aid and Home Nursing Lectures and discussed Nutrition with Doctors from overseas. Only Honorary Member of the Officers' Mess (Doctors and Psychiatrists, of 101 Convalescent Homes, the Largest Rehabilitation Centre in Great Britain.

Looked after 10,000 RAF and the US Flying Fortresses until the American Red Cross arrived.

Studied nutrition of the troops and the conditions in the Prisoner of War Camps.

As Lady County Welfare Officer of Bedfordshire and Voluntary Junior Commander (Captain) ATS, dealt with innumerable complaints over food from RAF Camps, Secret Stations and Searchlight Posts and with the health and employment of pregnant mothers from all three Services. Studied conditions in the hospitals treating the women in the Armed Services.

1945 Was introduced in America to the first B-Complex Multi-Vitamin (synthetic) capsule. On return home was closely in touch with the American manufacturers of Vitamins, receiving regular reports, literature and supplies until the Organic Vitamin Company opened at Hemel Hempstead.

1950 Vitamins saved her life. Kept fifty-two farrowing sows on her farm in Hertfordshire and experimented by giving them and the boars Brewers Yeast from a Brewery. For four years held the record production for Great Britain with an average of eleven a litter. Method copied by Sir Harry Haig for Ovaltine. Her prize-winning bull was given Vitamin E injections.

1955 Published: *Marriage for Moderns*, *Be Vivid*, *Be Vital*, *Love, Life and Sex*, *Vitamins for Vitality*, etc. Began her lectures on Health.

Became a County Councillor of Hertfordshire, on Education and Health Committees for nine years.

Studied nutrition with regard to school meals. Deeply concerned with the health and conditions of Old People. Was so horrified at the way they were fed in some Homes, and their general treatment, that her daughter (then Viscountess Lewisham) visited 250 Homes all over Great Britain. Following her reports and Barbara Cartland's and the tremendous press publicity involved, the Minister for Housing and Local Government (The Rt Hon. Duncan Sandys, MP) instigated an enquiry into the 'Housing and Conditions of the Elderly'.

Was on the Managerial Committee of several Old People's Homes and a Patron of Cell Barnes, the largest Home for retarded children in Great Britain.

Visited and inspected innumerable hospitals, clinics and Homes for the Elderly and children. Started her fight for better salaries and conditions for Midwives and Nurses, which brought her into close contact with many of the teaching hospitals and Royal College of Midwives.

1958 Was host to Pofessor Ana Aslan, founder of H3 on her first visit to England at the invitation of 400 doctors. Also tried Acupuncture and the Cyriac Method of holding a slipped rib or disc.

1960 Started to write monthly for *Here's Health*.

Co-founder of the National Association for Health.

Answered 5,000 letters a year – 10,000 in 1984. *The Magic of Honey* (1 million copies), doubled the sale of honey in Great Britain and over the world.

Lectured on Health to:

The Southgate Technical College

The Queen Elizabeth College of Nutrition

The Polytechnic

The Hertfordshire Police Cadets

Two lectures in the Birmingham Town Hall to audiences of 2,500

Frequent lectures to Midwives, Universities, Rotary Clubs etc.

1964-1978 Given a Civic Reception by the Mayor of Vienna for her work in the Health Movement.

Had private discussion on Health, herbs and health foods with: The Ministers of Health and Sciences in Mexico, Japan and India. Professors and Scientists in Mysore working on the development of agriculture in the famine areas near Kero with the India Ladies Committee and Officials on Health in Bombay, New Delhi and Mysore.

In touch with the Indian Guild of Service working among orphans, and in the poor areas in India, and saw the conditions among the first three million Pakistanis who moved into Calcutta in 1958.

Visited the new refugee areas in Hong Kong, was the first woman to visit (with the police) the Chinese border seeing the conditions of the workers.

Visited Nepal and saw the insanitary conditions in Katmandu and the rat-infested refuse in the streets. Discussed the conditions with officials.

Visited hospitals, clinics and old people's homes in many parts of India, Bangkok, Hong Kong, Singapore, Switzerland, Austria and France.

Taken on a special visit with five doctors and scientists to inspect the Vitel Clinic in France.

Visited the slums of Delhi, Calcutta, Bombay, Phnom-Penh (Cambodia), Tai-wan, Singapore, Rio, Harlem (New York), Glasgow, London, and had talks with the leading doctor in Istanbul and shown Clinical Trials undertaken.

Is closely in touch with the pioneers of the Health Movement in South Africa.

Invited – as a guest – to Yugoslavia, Germany and France.

1978 Visited Leningrad and Moscow and had talks with the Scientists on Old Age problems and the use of Ginseng.

1986 A Dame of Grace of St. John of Jerusalem: Chairman of the St. John Council, and Deputy President of the St. John Ambulance Brigade in Hertfordshire. One of the first women in 1,000 years to be on the Chapter General; President of the Hertfordshire Branch of the Royal College of Midwives: President of the National Association for Health.

AUTHOR'S NOTE

In England, the common-law guardianship, an outgrowth of feudal land law, conferred a right that it was profitable to the guardian. Only gradually did guardianship become a trust for the benefit of the ward. By the thirteenth Century, rights of wardship were recognised which enabled a feudal lord, upon the death of a tenant leaving an infant heir, to administer the tenant's estate as guardian during the heir's minority.

Over several centuries, guardianship, whether of the natural parent or other guardian, has slowly become recognised as including the right of custody of the child, control over education and religious training, consent to marriage, right of chastisement, right of enjoyment of his services, and control of his estate subject to the use of a sufficient portion for his education and maintenance.

By the Act of 1660 the father was given power to appoint by will or deed a guardian for his children to act after his death, and the mother was helpless to interfere with the father's appointment. Under provision of this Act, however, she could be designated as guardian if the father had made no appointment, or as joint guardian if he had, and she was also permitted to appoint a guardian to act after her death. Similar progress occurred regarding rights of custody.

In Europe the children's laws extended to the protection of life, prevention of ill-treatment or cruelty and a regulation of dangerous occupations, the imposition of employment restrictions, and the compilation of a great children's charter.

In England ill-treatment proscribed by law originally consisted of blows or threats, and was gradually broadened to include neglect to supply necessities. At the same time, children of well-to-do parents, however they were treated, found themselves powerless in the hands of their guardians, and the guardians' power to marry them when they were old enough was usually reinforced by the courts.

Chapter One
1818

Anybody seeing the Marquis of Raventhorpe driving his Phaeton would have been impressed.

With his high hat on the side of his dark head, his whip-cord coat fitting without a wrinkle, a cravat tied in a new style which had not yet reached St James's, he was the epitome of elegance.

At the same time, those who knew him well were aware that only a first-class tailor like Weston could conceal the muscles he had developed as an acknowledged pugilist in Jackson's Academy.

Hessians, shining like mirrors, covered his slim but very strong legs, on which he walked many miles in the pursuit of game-birds.

One might have thought that with his great entails, his enormous wealth, and a handsome countenance which made every woman in the *beau monde* long for his attention, the Marquis would have looked if not delighted with life, at least contented.

On the contrary, the cynical lines on either side of his firm lips and the fashionable droop of his eyelids made him appear disillusioned, as if he mocked at everybody he encountered.

He was well aware that while the younger Bucks copied his outward appearance, the older members of his Clubs shook their heads and said his arrogance and air of condescension showed that he was spoilt.

The Marquis, however, ignored all criticism and continued to live as he wished to do, winning all the Classic horse-races and maintaining, at his ancestral home, a perfection of organisation which infuriated the Prince Regent.

"I cannot understand, Raventhorpe," he said the last time he was staying with him, "why in your house I have better food, better attention, and certainly better wine than I have in my own."

There was a testy note in the Regent's voice which told the Marquis that he was jealous.

This was not surprising as he liked not only being considered the 'First Gentleman in Europe', but also to be first amongst his friends, and to excel, just as the Marquis did, at everything he undertook.

"I think the answer, Your Royal Highness," the Marquis replied, "is that you expect perfection, and that, Sir, even with your tremendous ability and perceptiveness, is almost impossible to find, especially where 'The Fair Sex' is concerned."

The Regent had laughed as the Marquis intended him to do, but when his visit was over he said to one of his other friends:

"I am damned if I will go there again in a hurry. I like to be at least on equal terms with my host, and not to feel that he is one up on me in every particular."

His friend, because he wished to toady for the Prince Regent's favours, expostulated that that was impossible.

Nevertheless it was something that was more or less acknowledged in the *beau monde*, and so indisputable that few people bothered to comment on it.

The Marquis was at the moment on his way to call on a young lady who he thought matched his ideal of perfection.

For years, in fact ever since he came of age, his relatives had been on their knees asking him to marry and to make sure that the Marquisate, which was of fairly recent creation, although the Earldom went back several centuries, continued.

The Marquis's two nearest relatives, first his brother and

then a cousin who had followed him as heir presumptive, had both been killed in the war against Napoleon.

It was therefore imperative that the Marquis should take a wife in case, by some unfortunate though unlikely accident, he was killed while fighting a duel, or broke his neck out hunting.

Alternatively he might catch one of the diseases so prevalent in London that the people had stopped worrying about them.

The Marquis, however, had declared he would never marry unless he found a woman who he thought was perfect enough to bear his name and sit at the head of his table.

The ideal of perfection stemmed from the fact that he had adored his mother, who had died when he was only seven years of age, but who had lived long enough to have remained in her son's mind as somebody beautiful, dignified, warm and loving.

Every woman he met, and the majority of them had made sure they did meet him, failed on one count or another to come up to his requirements.

But now, when his family and friends had almost despaired, he had met Lady Sarah Chessington and decided that she was in fact the most beautiful girl he had ever seen.

There were a number of people to tell the Marquis that they would make a perfect couple and that no two people could be more handsome, or in fact so exactly suited to each other.

Lady Sarah was the daughter of the Fifth Earl of Chessington-Crewe, whose horses continually tried to rival the Marquis's on the Race-Course.

His estate on the borders of Hertfordshire had been acquired only half a century after the Marquis's father had acquired theirs.

The Marquis's house had been completely rebuilt by the brothers Adam fifty years ago, but this did not detract from the fact that there was a mention of the land on which it stood belonging to a man named Raven in the Doomsday Book.

All this had persuaded the Marquis logically that Lady Sarah was the wife he was looking for.

He therefore, without hurrying himself in the slightest, had made it clear to her that she held his interest.

Lady Sarah had been fêted and acclaimed as an 'Incomparable' when she first appeared on the London scene, and that the Marquis should admire her was no less than what she expected.

She was, however, clever enough to look both surprised and flattered at his attention.

When he had finally decided that she possessed the attributes he required in a wife, he had notified her that he would be calling on her this afternoon.

After an early luncheon in his house in Berkeley Square, he had stepped into the Phaeton he had recently designed, and which had been a sensation from the moment he drove it down St James's Street.

It was not only smarter, better sprung, and more manageable than any other Phaeton ever seen, but it had an elegance that seemed part of the Marquis himself.

And the four horses which pulled it were a perfectly matched team which made all the horse-lovers in the Clubs grind their teeth as he passed.

Perched high behind on the small seat which always seemed somewhat precarious was a groom wearing the Marquis's livery and cockaded hat who always sat in the correct position with his arms folded and without moving, however fast his Master travelled.

It took the Marquis under an hour to reach the Earl's ponderous and rather over-spectacular iron gates which opened on to a long drive of oak-trees.

The Marquis could see the house in the distance and thought that architecturally it was an ugly building, and later additions to it badly designed.

At the same time it was undoubtedly impressive, and the

12

gardens surrounding it were well-cared-for.

He was aware however that the Earl had expended a great deal of money on buying a house in London in which to entertain for his daughter Sarah, the family mansion being too small for the Ball he gave for her, and for the Receptions which often involved entertaining two or three hundred guests.

The Marquis could not help thinking that if he married Lady Sarah as he intended to do, the Earl would feel such extravagance had been well worth while.

He knew that *débutantes* were dangled in front of eligible bachelors like flies over trout, but the snag was the very obvious hook of matrimony. Once the fish was caught there was no way of escape.

The Marquis, who had avoided many varied and ingenious baits over the years, could not help feeling that the Earl was a lucky man in catching the largest fish of them all.

It would have been mock modesty if he had not realised he had no equal amongst the bachelors of the *beau monde*, and there was no parent in the whole length and breadth of the land who would not have welcomed him as a son-in-law.

Lady Sarah had first attracted his attention at a large Ball given by the Duke and Duchess of Bedford, when in her white *débutante*'s gown she had looked, he thought, like a lily.

He had not, however, given her more than a passing glance, since he was at the time enjoying the company of the attractive wife of a foreign Diplomat who fortunately spent a great deal of his time travelling.

The Diplomat's wife was only one of several beautiful, witty and sophisticated women who passed through the Marquis's hands before he made up his mind to meet Lady Sarah.

Strangely enough he had found himself noticing her at every party, at every Assembly, and at every Ball he attended.

13

Each time he could not help thinking she was looking more beautiful than the time before, and that she had other attributes which he was sure were not to be found in most *débutantes*.

She moved with grace and without hurrying herself, her hands with their long, slim fingers were still, and not needlessly obtrusive, and when she spoke it was in a soft, low voice.

If there was one thing the Marquis disliked it was hard voices.

Several of his most ardent *affaires de cœur* had come to an end because he found that, however lovely a woman might be, if her voice irritated him he could no longer bear to be in her company.

His mistresses, who were too numerous and, as some wag had said, 'changed with the Seasons', came under the same criticism.

There was one entrancing little ballet-dancer he had set up in a house in Chelsea who was dismissed after only a few weeks because she had a hoarse voice in the morning which grated on His Lordship's sensibilities.

The road to Hertfordshire, being the main thoroughfare to the North, was kept in better condition than most other roads out of London.

The Marquis made good headway, so that he arrived at Chessington Hall a little earlier than he had expected.

There was, however, a groom waiting outside the front door to lead his horses to the stables.

Stepping down from his Phaeton the Marquis walked languidly up the red carpet, which had quickly been rolled down the stone steps, and through the front-door into the not very imposing Hall.

The Butler in a pontifical manner went ahead of the Marquis to show him into what he was aware was the Library, although it did not contain half as many books as did his own at Raven.

"I'm not certain, M'Lord," the Butler said respectfully,

"if Her Ladyship is downstairs, but I'll inform her of Your Lordship's arrival."

The Marquis did not reply, and thought a little cynically that Lady Sarah, anticipating his arrival, had doubtless been waiting eagerly at the top of the stairs. She would join him the moment she was officially informed he was there.

Slowly he walked across the room and as he reached the fireplace he noticed an indifferently painted picture of horses over the mantelshelf.

Then he was aware that a fire which had clearly been lit in the grate only a few minutes before was smoking badly, and the Marquis disliked smoking chimneys.

He took the greatest care at Raven and in all his other houses to have the chimneys swept every month during the summer, and every two weeks during the winter.

It was, he thought, quite unnecessary anyway at the beginning of May for a fire to have been lit at all.

As it had, it was unpardonable that it should have been allowed to smoke most unpleasantly.

As he knew the layout of the house, having been a guest of the Earl on several occasions in the past, when he did not have a *débutante* daughter on show, the Marquis left the Library.

He moved a little way down the passage to where there was, he knew, a room in which the Earl and Countess habitually sat when they were alone.

It opened out of the Blue Salon which was the main Receiving Room, and when there was a large dinner-party, it was often used as a card-room.

Cards were much more to his liking than the musical entertainment which so often took place after dinner in the country.

He had on various occasions won quite considerable sums from the Earl's guests, who were not as good or as lucky players as he was.

In this room, he noted, there was no fire, and he imagined with a slight amusement that Lady Sarah intended to receive him in the Blue Salon, which was a fitting background for her beauty, and also the right setting for a proposal of marriage.

While he was thinking of it, he heard voices and realised they came from the Blue Salon and that the door connecting it with the room he was in was ajar.

"But surely, Sarah," a girl's voice asked, "you are not going to keep His Lordship waiting?"

"That, Olive, is exactly what I intend to do," Lady Sarah answered.

The Marquis had no difficulty in recognising her voice. At the same time there was not the sweet softness about it which he had noticed particularly when she spoke to him.

"Why, Sarah? Why?"

He identified the other speaker now as a rather dull young woman he had encountered when he had attended a Reception which the Chessington-Crewes had given in Park Lane.

He had learned that her name was Olive, and he had vaguely remembered she was some relation.

As she was getting on for twenty-five, rather plain and, he thought, somewhat self-assertive, he had decided she was a bore and had moved away from her proximity as quickly as possible.

Now in answer to Olive's question, Lady Sarah said:

"It will do the noble Marquis good to cool his heels a little. He should have called on me at least three weeks ago, but as he has kept me waiting, I will now do the same to him."

"But, Sarah dear, are you wise? After all, he is so important and personally I find him very intimidating. Suppose, after all, he is not going to make you a proposal of marriage?"

"Nonsense!" Lady Sarah replied. "That is of course why he has come, and I consider it an insult that he has taken so long in making up his mind."

She paused before she said complacently:

"After all, as you well know, Olive, there is no one else

16

in the whole of London who is as beautiful as I am, and I have dozens of letters and poems to prove it."

"Of course, dearest," Olive agreed, "I am not disputing that, but unfortunately the Marquis has not written a poem to you."

"He is far too self-centred for that," Lady Sarah answered. "He is much more likely to write a poem to himself."

There was a little pause, then Olive said tentatively:

"But surely, Sarah dear, you are in love with him? Who could fail to be when he is so handsome and so rich?"

"That is the point," Lady Sarah replied, "so rich, Olive, and undoubtedly the most important bachelor in the whole of the *beau ton*."

"And therefore you love him!" Olive insisted.

"Mama says that love, such as you are talking about, is for housemaids and peasants. I am sure that His Lordship and I will deal well together, but I am not blind to his faults and I am certain he would not resort to threatening suicide, like poor Hugo."

"I should hope not!" Olive said quickly. "And what are you going to do about Hugo?"

Lady Sarah shrugged her shoulders.

"What can I do to cope with someone who loves me to distraction and says he would rather die than go on living without me?"

"But, Sarah, you cannot let him die."

"I doubt if he will do anything so silly. If he does, I shall be extremely annoyed. It would be sure to cause a scandal, and all those who are envious of me would be delighted to say I had encouraged him."

"I am afraid that is rather the truth."

"Poor Hugo," Sarah sighed. "I am sorry for him, but as you are aware, he could never offer me the Raventhorpe jewels or the position I shall have as a Marchioness."

"You will certainly be the most beautiful Marchioness there has ever been!" Olive enthused.

The Marquis, whose lips were set in a sharp line, decided he had heard enough.

He walked across the Sitting-Room and looked out into the passage, then quickly walked past the door into the Blue Salon and out into the hall.

There were two footmen on duty whispering together who sprang to attention as he appeared.

The Marquis passed them and walking down the steps set off towards the stables.

The footmen were so astonished at his behaviour that they made no effort to try to detain him.

He reached the stables to find his Phaeton standing in the centre of the cobbled yard while his groom and two stable-lads were giving his horses a drink from buckets spilling over with water.

The Marquis frowned before he climbed into his Phaeton, picked up the reins and, as his groom flung himself into the seat behind, drove off.

When he turned up the drive down which they had so recently come, he was furiously angry in a way he could not remember feeling for many years.

How could he, with his discrimination and what he had always thought of as his perception, have considered marrying somebody who could talk in a manner which had not only been unpleasant, but positively ill-bred?

He had prided himself for so long on being a good judge not only of horseflesh and men, but of women, too, that he was appalled at his own failure to realise that Lady Sarah, like so many of her sex, was interested only in a man's position.

She wanted the place he could give her in Society, not what he was in himself, which to him was of sole importance.

He was used to the sophisticated women with whom he had *affaires de coeur* losing their hearts irresistibly to him and loving him to distraction.

He could hardly believe that the young woman on whom

he had looked with favour should have considered him in such a cold, calculating manner.

He was genuinely shocked at the way she had spoken, and at the same time humiliated that he should not have been aware of what lay behind her beautiful face.

Like any young greenhorn, he told himself angrily, he had been captivated into believing a superficial beauty covered a heart of gold.

Perhaps even, an idea which was often laughed at, a soul.

It was something he wanted in the woman he would call his wife and who would be the mother of his children.

"How can I have been such a damned fool?" he asked himself furiously.

Only years of self-control prevented him from pushing his horses in his desire to get away from Chessington Hall with all possible speed.

"I will never marry – never!" he told himself.

He passed through the iron gates and set off down a side lane which would bring him out on to the main road.

He realised that in one aspect of the matter, he had had a very lucky escape, and he felt now like a man who by a hair's breadth had been saved from total destruction.

He was well aware that the fact that he had called at Chessington Hall and then not 'come up to scratch' would infuriate the Earl, and he could only hope it would upset and distress Sarah.

Although he felt contemptuous of any woman who would sell herself to the highest bidder, he knew he was more shocked than by anything else that he should have been so obtuse!

How could he have been so beguiled as actually to be prepared to offer marriage, which he had never done before, to a girl who was completely and utterly unworthy of bearing his name?

His chin was square, his lips were set in a tight line, and his eyes beneath his drooping eyelids were dark with anger as he drove on.

Then nearly a mile along the main highway he saw ahead, and there was no one else in sight, a small figure running along at the side of the road who turned to look back at the sound of his approach.

Then she deliberately stepped into the centre of the road and held out her arms.

He was surprised, but there was nothing he could do but pull his horses to a standstill only a few feet from the slight figure with her outstretched arms.

She had not moved, and had not in fact shown the slightest fear that he might run her down.

As the Phaeton came to a stop she ran to his side saying in a breathless little voice:

"Would . . you be very . . kind, Sir, and . . give me a lift?"

The Marquis looked down seeing a small, flower-like face turned up to his, dominated by two very large grey eyes that were surrounded by wet lashes which were accounted for by the tear-stains on her cheeks.

It was a very pathetic little face.

He could see that with the speed at which she had been hurrying along the road, her bonnet had been pushed on to the back of her head and her hair, which was curly, was rioting untidily over her forehead.

As he looked, wondering what he should reply, to his astonishment the girl, who was so young she seemed little more than a child, exclaimed:

"Oh . . it is . . you!"

"Do you know me?" the Marquis enquired.

"Of course, but I thought you would be with Sarah at the Hall."

The Marquis looked at her in astonishment. Then before he could speak the girl went on:

"Please . . please . . if you are going . . back to London . . take me with . . you . . if only a . . little way."

The Marquis realised now that she was not a village girl

as he had first thought, but spoke with an educated voice, and her reference to 'Sarah' told him that she must obviously have something to do with the Chessington-Crewe household.

"Surely," he said, "you are not going to London alone?"

"I have to! I cannot . . stand it any . . longer and if you will not take me . . I shall have to . . wait and find somebody else . . who will!"

There was a desperation in the young voice which made the Marquis say:

"I imagine you are running away and I will give you a lift on condition that you explain to me what you are doing and where you are going."

"Thank you . . thank you!"

Her eyes seemed suddenly to hold the sunshine in them.

She ran around the back of the Phaeton and without waiting for the groom who was getting down to help her, climbed up on the seat beside the Marquis.

"You are very kind," she said, "but I never expected it to be . . you when I heard your horses coming down the road."

The Marquis drove on slowly.

"I think you should start at the beginning," he said, "and tell me who you are."

'My name is Ula Forde."

"And you come from Chessington Hall?"

"Yes, I am living there or . . I was!"

There was a little break in the words, then she said quickly:

"Do not try to . . make me go . . back! I have made up my mind and, whatever . . happens to me . . it cannot be . . worse than what has been . . happening . . already."

"Suppose you tell me what it is," the Marquis suggested. "You must be aware that if I behave correctly, I should take you back."

"Why?"

"Because you are much too young to go to London alone, unless there is somebody there who is waiting to look after you."

"I will find . . somebody."

The Marquis thought dryly that this was very likely, but aloud he said:

"What has upset you so much at Chessington Hall that you have been forced to run away?"

"I . . I cannot stand being . . beaten by Uncle Lionel and slapped by Sarah and told that . . everything I do is wrong . . simply because they . . hated my father."

The Marquis turned his head and looked at her in complete astonishment.

"Are you telling me that the Earl of Chessington-Crewe is your Uncle?"

She nodded her head.

"Yes."

"And that he beats you?"

"He beats me because . . Sarah makes him . . and also because he will never forgive Mama for running away with my father . . but they were so happy . . so very, very . . happy . . and so was I . . until . . I came to my Uncle's house . . where it is exactly like being . . in Hell!"

The Marquis thought Ula must be deranged.

Then he realised she was not speaking in a hysterical manner, but in a sincere and collected tone of voice which made it difficult for him not to believe what she was saying.

"What was wrong with your father,' he asked after a moment's silence, "that made the Earl dislike him?"

"My mother . . who was his sister . . was very beautiful . . and she ran away with Papa the night before she was to be married to the Duke of Avon."

"And who was your father?"

"He was a Curate . . the Curate of the village Church of Chessington. Afterwards he became Vicar of a little village in Worcestershire . . where I was born."

"I can understand if your mother ran away the night before her marriage, it must have annoyed the family."

"They none of them ever spoke to Mama again . . but she was so happy with Papa that it did not matter, and although we were very poor and often had very little to eat . . we used to laugh and everything was wonderful . . until they were . . both k.killed last year in a carriage accident."

Again her voice was not hysterical, but the Marquis could hear the pain in it and realised how deeply it had upset her.

"It was then," she went on, "that Uncle Lionel came to the Funeral and . . when it was over . . he took me back with him . . and I have been miserable . . ever since."

"What have you done to make him angry?" the Marquis asked.

"He just hates me for being . . Papa's child . . and I cannot do anything that is . . right . . and it is not only the beatings . . and the slaps . . and Sarah pulling my hair . . but the fact that there is no . . love in that big house . . while our little Vicarage was always full of love . . like sunshine."

She was just stating a fact, the Marquis realised, and not trying to impress him in any way.

Then after they had driven a little further he asked:

"What made you run away today, particularly?"

"It was because you were coming to . . propose to Sarah," Ula said, "and everybody was in a fluster . . Sarah changed her gown several times to impress you . . and because she said I was slow at doing what she wanted . . she hit me with her hair-brush . . and told her mother I was being deliberately . . obstructive because I was . . jealous!"

Ula paused, then she went on:

"Aunt Mary said: 'Are you surprised? No one will ever marry Ula since she is without a penny to her name, and the

23

child of a common Parson who left a pile of debts because I expect he was even too stupid to think of paying them out of the Poor-Box!' ''

Ula gave a deep sigh.

"I suppose she thought she was making a joke, but I suddenly realised I could not . . bear it any longer . . and when Sarah hit me again . . I ran out of the room and out of the house . . and I swear I will never . . never . . go back!"

"What will you do with yourself?" the Marquis enquired.

"I intend to go to London and I intend to become a Cyprian!"

The Marquis was so astonished that he jerked the reins of the horses so that they threw up their heads.

"A Cyprian!" he exclaimed. "Do you know what you are saying?"

"Yes, I do. Cyprians have a lot of money given to them. Cousin Gerald, Sarah's brother, came home last week, and at first there was a terrible row because some of the tradesmen had written to Uncle Lionel to say he would not pay his debts and they intended suing him in the Courts."

She glanced up at the Marquis as she spoke to see if he was listening and she went on:

"He raged at Gerald for some time, then Gerald said: 'I am sorry, Papa, but I spent all my allowance on a very pretty little Cyprian. She asked me so nicely to give her what she wanted that I found it impossible to refuse her. I feel sure you understand.' ''

"And what did your Uncle say?" the Marquis enquired.

"He laughed and said: 'I do understand, my boy, and I felt the same when I was your age. Very well, I will settle these debts, but you are not to be so extravagant in the future.' ''

"So that made you feel you could be a Cyprian?"

"I . . I am not quite . . certain what they do," Ula

24

admitted, "but I am sure . . somebody will be able to tell me."

"And who do you intend to ask?"

She smiled at him and he thought as he looked at her again that she looked very like a small, rather badly treated angel who might have fallen out of heaven by mistake.

"Now that I have met you," Ula replied, "I can ask you!"

"And I will answer you," the Marquis replied. "It is quite impossible for you to be a Cyprian!"

"But . . why?"

"Because you are a Lady."

"Is there a rule that Ladies cannot be Cyprians?"

"Yes!" the Marquis replied without hesitation.

There was silence. Then Ula said:

"Then I shall have to find something else to do. Perhaps I could be a cook. I can cook very well, when I have the right ingredients.'

Before the Marquis could say anything she added:

"Perhaps I . . look rather . . young and people would hesitate . . before allowing me into their kitchens."

"I think that is undoubtedly the truth," the Marquis said, "but what would you like to do, apart from those two things?"

Ula gave a little laugh, and it was a very musical sound.

"What I would really like is . . quite impossible . . but it is to be an 'Incomparable' . . like Sarah . . and have all the attractive men at my feet . . begging me to marry them!"

"Then, I presume, you will choose the most important of them!" the Marquis said sourly.

Ula shook her head.

"Of course not! I would choose somebody I . . loved and who would love me . . but it is something which will never . . happen."

"Why should you say that?"

"Because, as Aunt Mary and Sarah have told me over and over again, no one will ever marry me because of the scandal Mama caused when she ran away with Papa . . and because I have no money . . not even a penny to my name!"

She gave a little sigh.

"It would be wonderful, even though Mama said it was vulgar, to be 'The Toast of St James's' with everybody thinking I was beautiful! But that is something that will never happen, so I just pretend it might in my dreams – and no one can take those away from me!"

"An 'Incomparable' like Sarah!" the Marquis said to himself.

Then when the traffic began to thicken on the road as they neared London, an idea came to him, an idea which made him look even more cynical than usual.

Now his eyes beneath his drooping eyelids were bright, at the same time dark, as if he was still angry, but working out a plan in his mind.

Chapter Two

They drove for a short while in silence. Then when the road was clear and Ula thought the Marquis would attend to her, she said:

"May I ask you . . something?"

"Of course."

"If you leave me in London, you will not . . tell Sarah where I . . have gone?"

"I shall not be seeing Sarah," the Marquis answered.

Ula looked at him in astonishment.

"But . . I thought . . I understood you were to . . propose to her this afternoon."

"I have not seen your Cousin, nor do I intend to do so," the Marquis replied, "and I have no intention of marrying her, or anyone else."

Now there was a note in his voice which told Ula he was very angry, and after a moment she said:

"Uncle Lionel will be very upset."

"That cannot be helped."

There was silence, then the Marquis said:

"I presume you are surprised that I have not proposed to your Cousin as everybody thought I intended to do."

"Everybody was so . . certain that was why . . you were calling," Ula replied. "At the same time, if you have . . really made up your mind . . not to marry her, I think you are . . wise."

"Why?"

He knew Ula was feeling for words before she said:

"I am sure that the only way for . . two people to be really . . happy when they are married is for them to . . love each other."

"Then you were aware that Lady Sarah did not love me?" the Marquis asked.

"Y . yes."

"She loves somebody called Hugo?" he questioned.

Ula shook her head.

"She used to laugh at his poems which were really quite beautiful, almost as good as Lord Byron's."

"She showed them to you?"

"No, she threw them away, and perhaps it was wrong of me to do so, but because they were so well written I . . kept them."

"You have not told me who this Hugo is."

"He is Lord Dawlish and I feel very . . very sorry . . for him."

"Why?"

The Marquis's sharp monosyllabic questions did not seem to perturb Ula and she answered:

"Because, although he loves Sarah with . . all his heart, she does not . . love him and would therefore . . if she married him, make him . . very unhappy."

There was a little pause. Then Ula said:

"They have said lots of strange things about you, and that you have . . no heart, but I do not believe that anyone who had so many fine horses would not . . love them."

The Marquis understood her reasoning and thought it something no one else had ever said to him.

After a moment he said:

"I think we must get down to your problem. As you have no one to love you or protect you, you will find London a very frightening and, in fact, a very dangerous place."

She looked at him a little apprehensively, then said:

"No one would steal anything from me, as I do not possess anything."

"I was not speaking of money," the Marquis replied.

"Then I cannot think what other dangers there are, except that Uncle Lionel may send the . . Bow Street Runners to look for me, although I think when Aunt Mary realises I have . . gone she will be glad."

"And what about your Cousin Sarah?"

"She hates having another girl in the house, even though I was treated as if I were a servant, and not allowed to . . come down to meals if there was . . a visitor."

"That seems extraordinary, considering you are your Uncle's niece!"

"As he told me so often, I am only a penniless orphan living on his charity and tainted for all time by . . my mother. I think really they were . . afraid that if anybody saw me the gossip would . . start all . . over again."

"I think that more than likely," the Marquis said, and now once again there was a calculating look in his eyes.

After driving a little further he turned off the main road and started to climb a hilly lane bordered by trees.

When they reached the top of it he turned in at some park gates with a lodge at the side of each gate, and Ula looked at him in surprise.

"Where are we going?" she enquired.

The Marquis pulled his horses to a standstill under the shade of a large lime-tree.

The horses were tired and therefore did not fidget unduly, and holding the reins loosely in one hand he turned halfway around in his seat so that he could look at Ula.

While they were driving she had tidied up her hair a little under her bonnet and he could see that like her Cousin Sarah's golden locks, it was fair, yet the very pale gold of the first fingers of dawn.

Her small face was heart-shaped and her eyes that seemed so unnaturally large in it were the soft grey of a pigeon's breast.

There was something very childlike about her, also, the Marquis thought, because she was so young and he was sure very innocent.

She seemed to exude a purity which made her look even more like a small angel than he had thought the first time he had looked at her.

As if she knew he was appraising her she looked at him.

While she raised her chin a little proudly as if she would not humble herself, at the same time there was a touch of fear in her eyes.

"I have something to suggest to you, Ula," he said, "and I want you to consider it very carefully."

"Yes . . of course," she answered, "but you do not mean to . . take me back?"

"It is what I ought to do," the Marquis replied, "but I have always disliked, in fact loathed, cruelty, though I find it hard to believe that anyone would treat a young girl as you say your Uncle and Cousin have done."

Ula's chin went up a little higher.

"Perhaps I ought . . not to have . . complained to a . . stranger, but I always tell the truth. Papa would have been . . very hurt if I had done . . anything else."

"Then of course I believe you," the Marquis said with a faint twist of his lips, "and that is why, Ula, I am not behaving as I should, and I will not take you back to Chessington Hall."

"Thank you . . thank you!" Ula cried. "I was afraid for one moment that was what you . . intended to do, and if I ran away, you could . . easily catch . . me."

"Very easily," the Marquis agreed, "but I do not want you to run away. I want you to help me, and at the same time yourself."

"Help you?" Ula questioned, but her eyes were shining and he thought the fear had left them.

"If you are upset by what you have experienced in your Uncle's house," the Marquis began, "I am also upset, though in a different way."

"What can they have done? What can they have . . said to you?" Ula asked impulsively. "The whole household was agog because you were coming to propose to Sarah.

30

Why did you not do so?"

"I do not intend to go into details," the Marquis said loftily. "It is sufficient for you to know that I learnt that your Cousin is very different from what I expected, and as I have already said, I have no intention of marrying her or, for that matter, anyone else!"

"You should never marry, unless you really fall in love," Ula said softly.

She thought the Marquis had not heard because he went on:

"It is something that is best forgotten, but I have an idea to which I am sure you will agree."

"What is it?" Ula enquired.

"It is that you should become the 'Incomparable' you have dreamed of being, and rival your Cousin by becoming the most talked about and admired woman in the whole of Society!"

Ula stared at him and her eyes opened so wide that they seemed to fill her whole face.

Then quickly she looked away saying as she did so:

"You are teasing me because it was . . very presumptuous of me to think of such a thing . . even in my . . dreams."

"I am not teasing you," the Marquis contradicted, "in fact I intend to make your dream come true."

Now she was looking at him again and she said:

"What are . . you saying? I am afraid I am being . . very stupid, but I do not . . understand."

For a moment the Marquis's lips were hard and set in a tight line.

Then he said:

"I intend to teach your Cousin a lesson, and your Uncle also, for his behaviour towards you is completely unpardonable."

He thought as he spoke that only a brute without any sensitivity could beat anything so fragile and fairy-like as the child sitting looking at him with wide eyes.

Her skin was very white, with the translucence of a pearl, and the Marquis found himself shuddering at the thought of a whip being applied to anything so delicate or so beautiful.

Because he knew Ula was waiting for his explanation he said:

"We are now in the drive of the house of my grand-mother, who is the Dowager Duchess of Wrexham. She is old, but still energetic and finds time heavy on her hands."

His voice was very firm as he went on:

"I am going to ask her to present you to the Social World, and especially to make it apparent to those who never have enough to gossip about that I consider you, without exception, the most beautiful person I have ever seen."

"They will . . think you are . . crazy!" Ula cried. "How can I possibly . . compare with anyone like Sarah, or indeed the . . beautiful women whom you . . admire?"

There was a hesitation before the last word and the Marquis asked sharply:

"Who has been talking about me, and what do you know about the women I 'admire'?"

Ula gave a little laugh.

"Everybody talks about you, you must be aware of that! When there were dinner-parties at Uncle Lionel's house I used to creep into the Minstrel's Gallery where no one could see me to watch the party down below. Sooner or later they always talked about you – the men about your horses, the ladies about your latest love-affair."

The Marquis did not speak and after a moment she said in a low voice:

"I . . I am sorry if it annoys you . . but you did ask me . . and actually it is a . . compliment that they think you are so . . important."

"It is a compliment I can do without!" the Marquis retorted. "Now, let us get back to you."

"But you . . cannot be . . serious," Ula said. "How could I possibly appear as someone . . beautiful? Even if you were kind enough to pretend that you . . thought I was

was, people would . . just laugh."

"I pride myself," the Marquis said, "on having a very discerning eye. If I saw an uncut, unpolished stone lying in the gutter, I hope because I am an expert on such matters I would know it was a diamond."

He knew Ula was listening intently and he went on:

"The same applies to a picture that is dirty or damaged, and has been allowed to deteriorate. I should still recognise it as a Rembrandt or a Rubens, however blackened it might have become with neglect."

"But . . that is quite different," Ula objected.

"Not really," the Marquis replied, "and I consider myself an expert on beautiful women. What you need, Ula, is a frame which will exhibit you to the best advantage, and also, like an actress on the stage, you need a Producer."

Ula clasped her fingers together as she said:

"You make it . . sound just possible . . but I find it hard . . to . . believe you."

"I think what you have to do is to trust me," the Marquis said. "As I have already said, if you achieve what you desire, you will at the same time help me to achieve what I want."

There was a hard expression in his eyes as he remembered how Sarah had spoken of him, and he said:

"With my reputation, my authority and my wealth, if we cannot make Social London accept you at my valuation, then all I can say is that I shall consider myself a failure, and that will be something that has never happened to me before."

"You have never failed at anything," Ula said. "Your horses win all the big races, and I have heard Uncle Lionel talk enviously of the magnificence of your house in the country which even the Prince Regent described as having 'an inconceivable perfection'."

The Marquis gave a short laugh.

"So that story has been repeated in your hearing!"

"I have already said that everybody talks about you and

everybody admires you."

"And do you?"

"That is a silly question! How could I not admire anyone who has been clever enough to find four horses as perfectly matched as these you are driving now?"

The Marquis thought with a slight twist of his lips that it was rather a different compliment from those he usually received, but he merely said:

"In which case, I must ask you again to trust me, and to do exactly what I tell you to do."

"And suppose I . . fail you and you are . . very angry with . . me?"

"I may be angry," the Marquis replied, "but I promise I will not beat you. In fact if you do fail, it will be my failure too, which I shall find extremely humiliating."

"That is something . . which must . . not happen," Ula said passionately. "I could not imagine you . . humiliated or anything but an autocrat sitting on top of the world . . eclipsing . . everybody else . . below you."

"Thank you," the Marquis said, "and just remember that you have to maintain me in that position and not let me, like Humpty Dumpty, have a great fall!"

Ula gave a spontaneous little laugh, and picking up the reins the Marquis drove on.

It was only as they came in sight of an attractive stone house with a porticoed front-door and long windows looking out over a garden brilliant with flowers that Ula was nervous.

The Marquis did not comment upon it.

He was however aware of the tension in her slim body and that her hands in her lap were clasped together so tightly that the knuckles showed white.

It struck him for the first time that she had run away without gloves, in fact, without taking anything at all with her.

She was dressed in a plain gingham gown, and she had over her shoulders a woollen shawl which looked as though it had been through innumerable washings.

At the same time, he was aware that her face glowed with a beauty that was not lessened by the plain ugly bonnet which was tied under her chin with frayed satin ribbons.

He liked the way when he lifted her down from the phaeton that she straightened her back and held her head high as she followed him into the house.

The old Butler with white hair beamed at the Marquis.

"Good afternoon, M'Lord! This is an unexpected pleasure! I know how delighted Her Grace'll be when I tell her that Your Lordship's here."

"How is Her Grace?" the Marquis asked, handing his hat and driving-gloves to one of the footmen.

"Well, very well, but if Your Lordship wants the truth, I thinks Her Grace is bored."

"That is something I have come to remedy," the Marquis said. "Will you take Miss Forde upstairs, Burrows, and ask your wife to show her where she can tidy herself while I have a word with Her Grace?"

"Of course, M'Lord, of course."

Taking command of the situation, which was somewhat unusual, he said to Ula:

"Will you wait here, Miss?"

Then he walked across the hall to open the door into the Drawing-Room.

"The Marquis of Raventhorpe, Your Grace!" he announced.

Ula heard somebody give an exclamation of delight before Burrows shut the door and returned to her.

The Marquis walked slowly across the exquisite Aubusson carpet to where his grandmother was sitting in an armchair beside the fireplace.

The Duchess of Wrexham had been the greatest beauty of her day, and her marriage to the Duke had been the most memorable social occasion of the year.

She had then become a leading hostess, and the parties

and Balls given by the Duke and Duchess at Wrexham House had often been attended by the King and Queen as well as other members of the Royal Family.

Now that she was over seventy she found the quiet life she lived in the country very dull, after being fêted, acclaimed and sought after not only by everyone of importance in England, but also in Europe.

She was still beautiful, although her hair was white.

As the Marquis appreciated, despite the fact that she was not expecting visitors, she was very elegantly gowned and was wearing some of the fabulous jewels her adoring husband had showered on her year after year.

"Drogo!" she exclaimed. "What a delightful surprise! Why did you not let me know you were coming? The least I could have done was to 'kill the fatted calf'!"

The Marquis laughed as he bent down to kiss his grandmother's cheek.

Then pulling up a chair beside her he said:

"I have come to ask for your help, Grandmama."

"My help?" the Duchess enquired. "I thought you had come to tell me you were going to marry that girl who has been so much talked about, Sarah Chessington."

"No, I have not come to tell you that," the Marquis said, "but actually to enquire if you remember somebody of the same name who was Sarah's Aunt, and who I believe caused a great scandal nineteen or twenty years ago."

The Duchess looked at her grandson in surprise.

"Are you referring to Lady Louise Chessington who ran away the night before her marriage to the Duke of Avon?"

"You remember it?"

"Of course I remember it," the Duchess said. "You never heard such a commotion as there was at the time!"

She chuckled as she said:

"It certainly took Avon down a peg or two. He was very puffed up with his own consequence, and assumed that any woman would die with joy at the idea of being his wife!"

"Did you ever meet Lady Louise?"

"Of course I met her! Her father was the Fourth Earl. He was an intelligent man, and actually, if you want the truth, he fell in love with me, and my poor, adoring husband was very jealous! But then he always was if any man so much as looked at me!"

"Who could help doing that, when you are so beautiful?" the Marquis asked.

"Thank you, Drogo. But I am too old for compliments now, although I am still delighted to talk of those I received when I was young."

There was a wistful note in the Duchess's voice and the Marquis said:

"I have a story to tell, Grandmama. But first I intend to tell you the truth about something which has just happened, and it is something I would not relate to anybody else."

The Duchess's eyes brightened and there was a note of curiosity in her voice as she asked:

"What has happened? I am also very curious to know why you are interested in Lady Louise?"

"That is what I am going to tell you . . " the Marquis replied.

When he had finished speaking and the Duchess had not uttered one word from the moment he started, the Marquis's voice, which had been quiet and almost devoid of emotion, suddenly had a note of anger in it as he added:

"That is why, Grandmama, I have brought this child, Lady Louise's daughter, who has been beaten and most inhumanely treated because of her mother's sins, here to you."

He had already related how he had picked up Ula in the road, and the Duchess did not seem surprised at the story but merely asked:

"And what do you expect me to do?"

"I will tell you exactly," the Marquis replied. "I intend to teach both her Cousin Sarah and her Uncle the Earl a lesson they will never forget."

His voice was sharp as he continued:

"To do so, I want you, Grandmama, to dress her and make her into the beauty her mother was. I want you to present her to the Social World in a way that will make her not merely rival, but eclipse her Cousin."

The Duchess stared at him, but her eyes were twinkling.

"A clever revenge, Drogo, if it is possible to pull it off."

"That is up to you, Grandmama, and I know of no one who could do it better."

"Is the child beautiful enough?"

"She is certainly unusual," the Marquis said, "but not in the same mould as her Cousin."

"That at least is helpful, and I have never known you stake your reputation on an outsider who did not win."

"There might always be a first time," the Marquis said, "but I shall be very disappointed if I am not first past the winning-post on this occasion."

"Then let me look at your entry," the Duchess smiled.

"I expect Burrows had the sense to wait until you were ready to see her," the Marquis replied.

He rose as he spoke and walked across the room.

As he opened the door, he saw Ula in the hall inspecting one of the pictures while Burrows was explaining to her the story of how it had come into the family.

When the Marquis appeared Ula looked at him with an expression he knew was one of delight.

At the same time before she moved towards him she said to the Butler:

"Thank you for all the things you have shown me. I have enjoyed it very much."

"It's been a pleasure, Miss," Burrows replied, and Ula ran towards the Marquis.

"I thought you wanted to be with your grandmother alone, so I did not interrupt."

"My grandmother is now ready to see you," the Marquis replied.

He saw a little quiver go through her and added:

"Do not be frightened, she is going to help you as I knew she would."

They walked into the Drawing-Room and the Marquis was aware that his grandmother was regarding Ula with a critical eye as she moved towards her.

Then as she reached her and Ula curtsied, she smiled and said:

"I am delighted to meet you, my dear. I knew your mother and you are very like her."

"You knew Mama?' Ula exclaimed with a lilt in her voice. "Then you must have known her when she was such a sensation in London, and people would wait outside the house for hours just to catch a glimpse of her."

"That is true," the Duchess confirmed, "but apart from her looks, everybody loved her for herself."

"Thank you for telling me that," Ula said, "and you will understand how much I miss her . . and Papa!"

There was just a little defiant note as she spoke of her father, as if she refused to allow him to be left out.

But the Duchess understood and she said:

"You must tell me all about them. I have often wondered if your father and mother were really happy, and whether it was worthwhile giving up the important position your mother would have had as the wife of the Duke of Avon."

"Mama once told me that she was the luckiest and happiest woman in the whole world because she had been fortunate enough to find Papa," Ula replied. "Even when things were difficult and we were cold in the winter because we could not afford enough coal she used to laugh and say:

" 'Nothing really matters as long as I have Papa and you, dearest, for that makes the house, even if it is as cold as Siberia, a little . . corner of Heaven because we are all . . together.' "

There was a break in Ula's voice as she spoke and it was with an effort that she forced back the tears from her eyes.

The Duchess put out a hand towards her and said:

"Sit down, child. I gather my grandson wants to plan how to make you the success your mother was, which I am sure she would want for you. I do not think it is going to be too difficult."

"Are you . . sure about . . that?" Ula asked. "His Lordship has the fantastic idea that I might be an 'Incomparable', but I know how plain I look compared with Sarah!"

She hesitated before she added softly:

"Papa said once that no one could be really beautiful unless they had the 'Divine Light' shining from inside them. Perhaps that is something I have not got, and only God . . could give it to me."

She spoke earnestly without the least embarrassment, and the Marquis watched to see what his grandmother's reaction would be to this very unusual young woman.

However, the Duchess did not appear to think what Ula had said was in the least odd. She simply replied:

"I think we shall just have to hope that you and I together can please my very fastidious grandson and make sure, as he has just said, that you gallop past the winning-post ahead of all the other competitors in the race."

Ula laughed, and the sound seemed to ring out around the room.

"Is that what I am to do?" she asked the Marquis. "Then I do hope I win the Gold Cup, as you did at Ascot last year."

"I am prepared to bet on it!"

"Please . . do not be too . . confident," Ula said quickly. "You might lose your money."

"Talking about money," the Duchess interposed, "the first thing Ula will require is the right clothes."

Ula gave a cry of protest.

"I had forgotten that! Oh, please, Ma'am, I am sure you realise I should not allow His Lordship to pay for my gowns, but when I ran away in such a hurry I brought nothing with me."

There was a worried expression on her face as she turned to the Marquis and said:

"I cannot be an . . encumbrance on . . you . . or on Her Grace."

The Marquis rose to his feet to stand with his back to the fire.

"Now let me make it clear from the very beginning," he said, "that I cannot have my plans interfered with. As you promised, Ula, to trust me, you must also obey me."

Ula's eyes fell before his. Then she said in a low voice:

"Mama . . told me once that a Lady could only . . accept small presents . . from a gentleman without being thought 'fast', or . . improper. I think she meant a fan or perhaps a pair of gloves . . nothing else."

"And yet I think you had originally very different ideas of what you would accept when you came to London!" the Marquis remarked.

Ula blushed and looked very lovely as she did so. Then she said:

"I . . I thought then I should be . . earning the money not . . just accepting it as a . . gift."

"That is the answer!" the Marquis said. "You will be earning the money because you will be carrying out my orders and you can, if you like, think of me as being your employer."

For a moment Ula considered this.

Then she looked at the Marquis in a mischievous manner and he realised she had a dimple on each side of her mouth.

"I am sure Your Lordship has just thought of that idea on the spur of the moment but, as it saves my face, I shall accept it and say thank you very much!"

The Duchess laughed.

"I have always told you that you are extremely ingenious, Drogo, when it comes to getting your own way. You were just the same when you were a small boy."

"I am sure he is very clever," Ula said, "because he always seems to have the answer to everything."

"I agree with you," the Duchess smiled, "and now, Drogo, what are your orders?"

"They are quite simple," the Marquis replied. "Ula will stay here the night with you and, as I expect you will retire early to bed as you usually do when you are in the country, I will dine with her, and give her some last-minute instructions. Tomorrow you will both come to Berkeley Square."

"Tomorrow?" the Duchess queried. "But what about her clothes?"

"She will of course not be seen until you have fitted her out, and it is important she should look at least presentable within at most twenty-four hours."

The Duchess gave a little scream.

"That is quite impossible!"

"Nothing is impossible," the Marquis said. "Today is Sunday. Tomorrow evening as soon as you arrive you will send out invitations to a small reception for your intimate and most important friends to meet Lady Louise's daughter."

Ula gave a little exclamation and the Duchess stared at her grandson. He saw the question in her eyes and he said:

"You knew Lady Louise and you were very fond of her. Now that she is dead, you wish to show your affection and your admiration for someone who gave up the social world for the man she loved by presenting her daughter to the *beau monde*."

The Duchess smiled.

"Drogo, you are a genius! Nothing could intrigue or excite people more than first to learn that Louise had a daughter, and secondly that she is under my chaperonage and in your house."

"That is exactly what I thought," the Marquis agreed.

"Will they not still be . . shocked at the . . scandal Mama caused by . . running away?" Ula asked haltingly.

"They will be intrigued and amused, and I am quite certain they will be full of admiration, as I am, for anyone who was brave enough to do such a thing," the Duchess said firmly.

"Uncle Lionel will be . . horrified!" Ula murmured.

"I hope so!" the Marquis said. "In fact the more horrified he is, the better I shall be pleased!"

He paused and looking into Ula's troubled eyes he added:

"What you have to do is to forget what you have suffered at his hands and your Cousin Sarah's. You are starting a new life, Ula, and I think you will find it a very exciting one."

"I only . . wish Mama could . . thank you, as I am . . trying to do," Ula said. "I can only . . think that I am . . dreaming, and in the . . morning I shall . . wake up."

The way she spoke made the Duchess laugh, but once again Ula was forcing back the tears from her eyes.

She went upstairs to have a bath before dinner when the Duchess retired to bed.

"I am going to need all the rest I can get, dear child," she said, "because once we are in the thick of the entertainments which will be arranged for you, I have every intention of enjoying myself by being present at all the Balls, and by accepting all the other invitations which will be showered upon us."

Ula gave a little laugh and the Duchess, as she kissed her cheek, said:

"Leave everything to Drogo. He loves a challenge and he will enormously enjoy making plans and embarking on a campaign as if he were a General. All we have to do is to follow his orders."

"You have both been so kind," Ula said. "Last night I went to bed in tears because Uncle Lionel had beaten me again, and Sarah had pulled my hair. I . . I wanted to die . . but now I want to live because . . everything is so . . exciting!"

"That is exactly what it is going to be for both of us," the

Duchess smiled and went into her own bedroom.

Later, just before he was going down to dinner, the Marquis came to say good night to her.

Lying against her lace-edged pillows, her grey hair covered with a very becoming little lace cap, and lace falling over her hands from her silk nightgown, the Duchess still had a shadow of the beauty that had been hers in the past.

There was an expression of satisfaction in her eyes as she looked up at her grandson.

In his evening-clothes the Marquis was unbelievably elegant.

He was wearing instead of knee-breeches and silk stockings, the long tight-fitting black drainpipe trousers which had been invented by the Prince Regent.

His cravat was tied with great ingenuity, and his tail-coat with its silk lapels had been cut by a master-hand.

With his hair in the windswept fashion, again introduced by the Prince Regent, the Marquis looked so handsome that the Duchess wondered how any girl could have been such a fool, as Lady Sarah had been, as to lose him.

At the same time she was well aware that the cynical lines running from his nose to his lips were even deeper than usual.

She was sure that not only his eyes were critical of everything and everybody, but his whole attitude was more supercilious than ever.

"Curse the girl!" she said to herself. "She had the chance of sweeping away the disillusionment that spoils him, and whatever he may say it will take him a long time to forget and forgive!"

She did not however voice her thoughts aloud, and merely exclaimed:

"How smart you look, Drogo dear! No wonder the Prince Regent is jealous of you when he grows fatter and fatter year by year, while you seem to grow slimmer."

"That is because of the exercise I take," the Marquis

replied. "Besides, I do not gorge myself as everybody has to do at Carlton House night after night!"

"Nevertheless your Chef at Berkeley Square is an excellent man," the Duchess replied, "and I look forward to enjoying my meals as your guest."

"It will be delightful to have you," the Marquis said quite sincerely.

"Do you really mean to say I have only twenty-four hours in which to make that child a sensation?" the Duchess asked.

"It is best to 'strike while the iron is hot'," the Marquis answered, "and you must be aware that once Ula is launched under your chaperonage it will be impossible for the Earl to make any claim to take her back to the country."

"I understand," the Duchess said, "and that is something which must never happen."

She looked up at the Marquis as she added:

"My lady's-maid tells me that when she helped Ula with her bath, she was appalled by seeing the scars on her back, some of which were still bleeding from the beating she received last night!"

The Marquis frowned.

"Then it is true what she told me?"

"Only too pitiably true," the Duchess said. "Robinson says she must have suffered agonies not only when it happened, but also when the open wounds stuck to her clothing, which had to be pulled away when she undressed."

The Duchess saw with satisfaction the anger in the Marquis's eyes and the tightness of his lips.

She knew that he had rather doubted Ula's story of how her Uncle had beaten her, and she had had the same suspicion herself.

But there was now no doubt that the child had been treated even worse than any drunken labourer would have treated his children after drinking on a Friday night.

"I will see that Chessington-Crewe pays for this!" the Marquis said.

"I can only thank God," the Duchess said quietly, "that you have been spared a marriage which would have made you not only unhappy, but even more cynical and disillusioned than you are already!"

"Who said I am either of those things?" the Marquis asked truculently.

"I am not going to argue about it," his grandmother replied. "As you were always my favourite grandson, all I have ever wanted for you is that you should find happiness."

"I have no hope that will prove possible," the Marquis said, "but I am prepared to settle for a certain amount of contentment and that, at the moment, certainly does not include marriage."

As if he did not wish to say any more, he kissed his grandmother's cheek, then her hand.

"Good night, Grandmama!" he said. "I am exceedingly grateful to you for playing my game with such charm and grace, and whatever happens, you will delight in watching two people who are quite despicable getting their just deserts."

He smiled at her and went from the room.

But there was a sad expression on the Duchess's face as she remained looking at the door for some time after he had passed through it.

Chapter Three

The Marquis drew his gold watch from his waistcoat pocket.

"It is time for dinner," he said sharply. "You must teach Ula to be on time."

"I think," the Duchess replied, "she is delayed by the new gown I bought her in Bond Street this morning, and is hoping you will admire it."

The Marquis did not answer, and the Duchess went on:

"She certainly 'pays for dressing', as the servants say. In fact I am sure you are right, Drogo, in your confidence that she will be a sensation when she appears at my Reception tomorrow, and at the Ball you are giving on Friday."

The Marquis still said nothing, but the Duchess knew he was listening and after a moment she asked:

"You have heard nothing, I suppose, from Chessington Hall?"

"Why should I?" the Marquis enquired. "After all, what can they say, except that it was strange that I should call to see Lady Sarah and then disappear."

"They must have been disgruntled by your behaviour."

"That is what I hope!" the Marquis replied grimly.

He glanced at his watch once again, then looked at the Sèvres clock on the mantelshelf, as if he thought he might be mistaken in the time.

As he did so, the door opened and Ula came in.

The Duchess was expecting her to walk slowly and perhaps a little self-consciously in a new gown that was, she thought, one of the prettiest she had seen for a long time.

It had been a very tiring day, searching for clothes that were ready for her to wear or required only a few alterations.

In fact, when they returned home at teatime, the Duchess had gone to her bedroom to lie down and it had been quite an effort to come down to dinner.

She was however determined to see the expression on her grandson's face when he realised the little duckling he had brought her yesterday had undoubtedly turned into a swan.

In fact, experienced though she was in both beauty and the wearing of fashionable gowns, the Duchess could hardly believe, when she had seen Ula just before she came downstairs, that she was the same pathetic and frightened girl, shabbily dressed and with untidy fair hair, whom her grandson had brought to her.

Now Ula was wearing a gown which fitted her to perfection, and revealed the exquisite lines of her figure.

The tight bodice was ornamented with the decorations which were the vogue after the long years of austerity during the war.

The gown which the Duchess had taken so much care in choosing was of white gauze faintly sprinkled with a touch of silver which made it shimmer.

It was decorated with snowdrops that had *diamanté* like dewdrops on their petals.

They nestled in the chiffon which encircled the *décolletage*, and made Ula look more than ever like a small angel who had just peeped through the fleecy clouds in a summer sky.

Her hair, instead of rioting over her forehead as it had when the Marquis had first seen her, had been dressed by the most experienced hairdresser who served the *beau monde*.

He had, when he had finished, exclaimed with delight that his new client was as beautiful as Diana the Huntress.

To the Duchess's surprise, however, Ula did not attempt to show off her gown as she came into the Drawing-Room.

Instead she ran with almost undignified haste towards the Marquis.

"I am sorry . . I am . . sorry," she said a little breathlessly. "I know I am late for dinner, but your knife-boy had an accident and cut his hand very badly. No one knew what to do until I . . bandaged it with . . honey."

The Marquis looked at her in astonishment.

"My knife-boy?"

"Yes, he cut himself in the kitchen and was crying with the pain. When I was told what had happened I knew what should be done, so I had to go to him."

"You have been in the kitchen!" the Marquis said slowly as if he could hardly believe it himself.

"Willy – that is his name – is much better now," Ula said, "but he is very frightened in case you should dismiss him for being so careless. But you will not do that . . will you?"

She looked up, her blue eyes pleading with him.

There was a silence.

The Marquis intended to say that his secretary dealt with all household affairs and, apart from giving exact orders as to what he required, he never interfered.

Then, as he found it impossible not to respond to anyone so ingenuous, he answered:

"No, of course not. He could not help having an accident."

Ula gave a cry of delight.

"That is what I knew you would say, and I must tell Willy not to worry any more."

Without waiting she turned and ran from the room, leaving the door open behind her.

The Marquis turned to look at the Duchess and saw that she was laughing.

"Society beauties," he said severely, "should not go into kitchens or concern themselves with knife-boys."

"I know," the Duchess replied, "but Ula is different.

Very different, I may add, from that beauty with whom you were so busy at one time – let me see – what was her name? Lady Salford."

She laughed before she continued:

"If you remember, after she had given a footman notice and he cut his throat, she merely remarked: 'I hope he has not spoilt the carpet!' "

The corners of the Marquis's mouth twitched as if he could not help it, but before he could reply to his grand-mother, Ula came back.

She had run so quickly, knowing that she was keeping the Marquis from his dinner, that now her elegantly coiffured hair was slightly ruffled and little curls had reappeared on her forehead.

"He is very . . grateful," she said, breathlessly as she reached the Marquis. "In fact he said: 'I always knows His Nibs were a real sport!' "

The Duchess laughed.

"You cannot expect a fairer compliment than that, Drogo!"

"Dinner is served, M'Lord!" the Butler announced from the doorway.

The Marquis helped the Duchess out of her chair and offered her his arm.

Following behind them towards the Dining-Room Ula thought that everything was more exciting than she could possibly have imagined.

Because there had been such a drama with the knife-boy's hand, she had forgotten her gown.

Now as they passed down the corridor she saw herself reflected in a gilt-framed mirror.

She also saw that her hair was untidy and put her hand up to smooth the curls back into place.

Then when they were in the Dining-Room she again forgot her own appearance as she realised how impressive the Marquis looked sitting at the top of the table in a high-backed chair.

She was also thrilled to see the polished table without a cloth which she had heard was a fashion introduced by the Prince Regent.

On it were some magnificent gold ornaments, the candelabra each bearing six candles, and the table was also discreetly decorated with orchids.

Everywhere she looked there was a beauty which appealed to her in a way the large but ugly rooms at Chessington Hall had never done.

For the first time since her parents' death she felt she was not despised or ignored, and that she was being treated as an ordinary guest by two very kind and distinguished people.

As if the Marquis knew what she was thinking he said:

"I hope everything meets with your approval."

"It is just how your house ought to look," she replied.

"What do you mean by that?"

"Grand, because that is what you are, and at the same time beautiful. There is also something warm and kind about this room and in fact the whole house, which I have not found for over a year."

"I think perhaps, Drogo, that is the nicest compliment you have ever been paid," the Duchess said. "And it is true that I always feel happy when I am in one of your houses."

"Thank you," the Marquis said, "and that is what Ula must feel in the future."

"It is wonderful for me to find it again," Ula replied.

He knew she was thinking how happy she had been when her father and mother were alive.

"Now we must make plans for the Ball," the Duchess said.

Listening to her discussing with the Marquis how many people they should invite, how the Ball-Room should be decorated, what they would have for supper, and which Band was considered best at the moment, made Ula think once again she must be dreaming.

None of this could be happening to her.

Deep down inside her there was a fear that at any moment she would be taken back to Chessington Hall.

The Marquis, however, was intent on making the Ball so important and so unusual in every particular that Lady Sarah would be furious that it was not given in her honour.

He had already told the Duchess that he intended to invite the Earl and Countess of Chessington-Crewe and Lady Sarah to be present.

"Is that wise?" she enquired.

"I want to see their faces when they learn the Ball is given for Ula."

There was something almost cruel in the Marquis's eyes as he spoke, and the Duchess said:

"Revenge is not always as gratifying as one hopes, Drogo!"

"I shall find it very gratifying," the Marquis replied, "and to make my revenge complete, you have to make Ula look much more beautiful and better-dressed than her Cousin."

"I will do my best," the Duchess said. "In fact, in my opinion, Ula is ten times more lovely than Lady Sarah, who I have always felt, whilst she has a classical perfection, has what my old maid used to call 'hard eyes'."

"I know that now," the Marquis said sharply.

They did not talk about it any more, but the Duchess was aware that he was still furious with himself for having been deceived by a beautiful face into believing that Lady Sarah loved him and would have made him a good wife.

The Duchess was well aware how many women had wanted to marry her grandson and how many more had been deeply and wholeheartedly in love with him.

She knew it had been for him a very bitter setback to realise that he had made a fool of himself.

She could only hope it would not make him more cynical about love than he was already.

Because she had always loved Drogo more than any of her other grandchildren, she had always hoped that he would find a girl to marry who would love him for himself, and not for his title and his very great possessions.

She could hardly imagine it possible that Lady Sarah should not have fallen in love with him as all the rest of her sex seemed to do.

It had disillusioned him to the point where he was wholly obsessed by the idea of taking his revenge upon her.

"And when he has done so," she asked herself, "where will it get him?"

It would certainly drive him back into the arms of the married, sophisticated women who in her opinion engaged far too much of his time, as well as his brains and money.

The Duchess, however, did not say anything about this to Ula when on the following day they once again went shopping.

On the way home, after it seemed to Ula they had bought up everything in Bond Street, she slipped her hand into the Duchess's and said:

"You do not think it wrong, Ma'am, that I should accept so much from His Lordship? I am sure Mama would be shocked. At the same time, as he thinks I am helping him, perhaps it is not wrong, as it would be if it was just for me."

"You are not to worry your head over the whys and wherefores," the Duchess said firmly. "Drogo is a law unto himself, and if he wants something he invariably gets it."

Her voice was very kind as she went on:

"All you have to do is to enjoy yourself, my child, and remember that you are a reflection of your mother, who shone like a star at every Ball she attended."

"I shall never be as beautiful as Mama," Ula said. "At the same time, I cannot help feeling she would be pleased that I have escaped from Chessington Hall."

She paused before she said:

"Last night I . . woke up and found I was . . screaming because I thought Uncle Lionel was . . beating me."

"Forget him!" the Duchess said sharply. "There is no reason why he should frighten you any more, and he will not interfere in your life from now on."

There was silence, then Ula said in a very small voice:

"But . . what is to . . become of me . . when I am no longer of any . . use to His Lordship?"

"I have been thinking about that," the Duchess replied, "and I intend to ask him if you will come and live with me. You may find it rather dull, but I am sure, even if you are not living at Raventhorpe House, a great many of your admirers will call on us in Hampstead."

Ula gave a cry of delight.

"Do you really mean that? Are you quite . . sure you want me? . . You are not just being . . kind?"

"I would love to have you," the Duchess replied, "but I have a feeling that long before that you will be married."

Ula shook her head and the Duchess said firmly:

"Of course you will! In fact I shall consider it an insult if, having produced, with the help of my grandson, a new star in the social firmament, there are not at least a dozen eligible young men knocking on the door and laying their hearts at your feet."

The way the Duchess was speaking was so funny that Ula laughed.

"I am sure they will do nothing of the sort," she said, "but it would be very exciting to have even . . one proposal."

There were no proposals at the Reception which took place in the afternoon.

But wearing a very beautiful gown Ula received a great number of compliments from the Duchess's friends.

Most of them had known her mother, and all of them without exception remembered the sensation Lady Louise had caused when she ran away on the night before her wedding.

Before the Reception Ula had been a little afraid that some of the Duchess's friends might criticise or condemn her mother, in which case she would have found it difficult to be polite to them.

But without exception they all told her how beautiful her mother had been, and how brave it had been of her to marry the man she loved rather than the Duke chosen for her by her father.

"She was so different from the other girls of her age," one lady said, "and I am sure, my dear, that you are very like her."

"What made her so different?" Ula enquired.

The lady paused, then she said:

"I think it was that she was obviously so good in herself, that it was difficult, in spite of her beauty, for us to be jealous of her."

She smiled as she explained:

"She was always prepared to share everything, even the men who admired her, with the girls who did not have as many partners as she had. It would have been impossible to dislike anyone who was so warm-hearted and so lovable."

After all the cruelly unkind things her Uncle and Aunt had said about her mother, it gave Ula a warm feeling to hear people talk of her like that.

To the lady who had first spoken she said:

"Thank you very much for what you have said to me. I only wish Mama could . . hear you. She would be . . very proud."

Everybody to whom Ula talked asked the same questions.

Had her mother been happy, really happy? Had she no regrets at running away as she had?

"Mama and Papa were the happiest people in the world," Ula replied. "As for regrets, Mama always said she thanked God every day when she said her prayers for giving her Papa and letting her be brave enough to run away with him."

By the time the Reception was over the Duchess had

received a dozen invitations to luncheon and dinner-parties to which she was bring Ula.

Also the promise of invitations to several Balls which would arrive in the next day or so.

"You were a huge success, child," she said as the last guest departed and they were alone in the flower-filled Drawing-Room where the Reception had taken place.

"It was very exciting to hear all your friends saying such nice things about Mama," Ula said.

She looked at the Duchess, then asked in a small voice:

"Did I . . behave as you . . wanted me to? I did not do . . anything wrong?"

The Duchess put a hand on her shoulder.

"You did everything that was right, my dear," she said, "and I was very, very proud of you."

"You are . . sure, quite . . sure?" Ula persisted.

The Duchess understood that being abused and beaten and forced to endure the harsh criticism of her parents at Chessington Hall had made Ula unsure of herself.

"What you have to acquire, my dear," the Duchess said as they went from the Drawing-Room and started up the stairs, "is some of my grandson's arrogance. He is quite sure he is always right, and that, I think, is an asset in this world."

Her voice was mocking as she added:

"Especially in a society in which whatever one does or whatever one says, somebody is going to be critical. When they are, it is a mistake to let oneself be hurt by it."

"I understand what you are saying," Ula said, "but I cannot be as . . pretty or as . . successful as you say . . I am."

The Duchess laughed.

"That is not at all the right attitude! You have to learn to look down your nose and say: 'If they do not like me as I am, then they will just have to put up with me!' "

Ula laughed too.

"I doubt if I shall ever be able to do that."

"What are you laughing about?" a voice behind them said.

They looked around from halfway up the stairs to see that the Marquis had entered the hall.

"How did your party go?" he enquired.

"Need you ask?" the Duchess replied. "Your *protégée* was a huge success, but she is finding it hard to believe that the compliments she received were entirely genuine."

The Marquis looked up at Ula's flushed, flower-like face looking down at him over the banisters.

He thought as he did so that it would be impossible to find in the whole of London anyone so lovely in her unique manner.

He told himself he had been extremely clever in realising her potential when he had picked her up in the road.

As he walked away to his Study he was thinking with satisfaction of how he had just alerted the members of White's Club into being curious.

He had walked into the Coffee-Room and automatically, because it was his acknowledged right, had taken the place which had formerly been occupied by Beau Brummell in the famous bow-window which overlooked St James's Street.

"I thought you were in the country, Raventhorpe!" one of his friends remarked.

"I have returned," the Marquis said.

He knew as he spoke that quite a number of his closest friends were aware that he had gone to the country to see Lady Sarah Chessington.

Although he had not said so, they had instinctively assumed that he intended to propose to her.

They waited now for him to tell them when the wedding would take place, on the presumption that no woman would refuse such a matrimonial catch.

In fact the Marquis was aware the betting for the last week at White's had been four-to-one on his proposing to the incomparable Sarah.

There was silence until somebody asked a little tentatively, knowing how seldom the Marquis talked of his private affairs:

"Did anything happen while you were in the country?"

"It certainly did," the Marquis replied, "but I think it would be a mistake for me to tell you about it."

"Why the secrecy?"

"It will not be a secret for long," he answered. "In fact, I found myself quite unexpectedly in the role of explorer discovering an hitherto unknown, priceless jewel!"

The Marquis was well aware as he finished speaking that there was an extremely puzzled expression in his friends' eyes.

Two of them drew their chairs a little closer to his and another, bolder than the rest, asked:

"What do you mean – an *unknown* treasure?"

The Marquis knew he was thinking that while Lady Sarah might be an 'Incomparable' and was certainly a treasure, there was nothing unknown about her!

In fact, she had been the toast of all the Clubs in St James's for the past six months.

"Unknown to you and certainly to me until I found her. But I suppose that is what we are all seeking in one way or another," the Marquis said cryptically. "It is what has kept the poets raving, the artists painting, and the musicians composing ever since the beginning of time."

"What the devil are you talking about, Raventhorpe?" his friend enquired.

"Beauty," the Marquis said, "beauty that is untouched, unspoilt, and hitherto unacclaimed."

There was silence.

Then one of the Marquis's contemporaries who was rather more intelligent than the others asked:

"Are you telling us that you have found a new 'Incomparable' whom none of us has seen previously?"

"I should not have thought it difficult for you to understand plain English," the Marquis replied, "but if you do not believe me, then I suggest you accept the invitation you will receive from my grandmother, the Dowager Duchess of Wrexham, tomorrow for a Ball that will take place at my house on Friday night."

"A Ball?" someone exclaimed. "For an unknown beauty? Really, Raventhorpe, you never cease to surprise me!"

The Marquis rose from his chair.

"I am glad about that," he said, "for if there is one thing I find intolerably boring, it is the ceaseless repetition of the obvious. Someone new will give you something new to talk about!"

With that parting shot he walked out of the Coffee-Room leaving behind him a buzz of voices rising higher and higher.

He knew what he had said would be repeated in the Drawing-Rooms of London by the end of the evening.

It would be augmented by reports from the older members of the community who had attended the Duchess's Reception.

The Social World would be agog with curiosity long before the Ball on Friday night.

Only the Marquis with his genius for organisation could possibly have arranged everything with such unprecedented speed.

By some magical means of his own, the invitations were printed and his servants had delivered them all over London by luncheon-time the next day.

There was fortunately no other Ball of any great importance to be given on Friday night.

Even if there had been it was doubtful if anyone would have refused the Marquis's invitation while curiosity had mounted every hour of the following day.

Once the gossips were aware of who Ula was, the story of her mother's elopement became more and more romantic and more exciting every time it was repeated.

In a society where every girl's ambition in her first

Season was to find a husband with the highest possible title, the greatest possessions, and the most important position, what Lady Louise had done had been inconceivable at the time.

It seemed even more incredible now, that an undisputed beauty should have not only refused to marry the Duke of Avon but had done so at the very last moment.

Over five hundred people had been expected as guests at the wedding.

The Church had been decorated, the Archbishop of Canterbury was to marry them, and several members of the Royal Family were to be present in the congregation.

To leave all that and run away with the Curate of her father's parish in the country seemed unthinkable.

Daniel Forde was, in fact, the third son of a well-bred country gentleman who had no reason to be ashamed of his lineage.

His father was a third Baronet, but there was little money.

While Sir Matthew Forde could provide for his eldest son, who would succeed to the Baronetcy, and for his second to join a not too expensive Regiment, there was nothing left for the third.

Daniel therefore, because it was traditional, went into Church, although he would have preferred, if he had had the choice, to join the Navy.

He was not only strikingly good-looking and exceedingly charming, but he was also a man of great compassion and understanding of other people's problems.

It therefore turned out that he had made a remarkably good Parson.

He loved people for what they were and not for what they pretended to be.

He found the difficulties and worries of his flock became his personal problems, so that he exercised his brain as well as his heart in doing his best to solve them

It was obviously impossible for him to return with Lady

Louise to Chessington Village after they had run away.

His father therefore in consultation with the Bishop who, fortunately, was an old friend, arranged for Daniel to be appointed Vicar to a small village in Worcestershire.

It was assumed that their presence there would offend no one, and their social crime would soon be forgotten.

Actually there was very little social life in their new parish, which suited Lady Louise who wanted only to be alone with the man she loved.

They were supremely happy with their only child until, as Ula grew older and, as her mother saw, very lovely, she wondered how it would be possible for her ever to meet the right sort of man whom she could marry.

There was however no chance of her being forgiven by her own family for refusing to marry the Duke, and Daniel's father was now dead.

His two elder brothers were both struggling to live on small incomes with a number of sons each of whom demanded an education which they found very expensive.

"If only Ula could have a Season in London," Lady Louise had said once to her husband.

Then she regretted she had spoken.

It still hurt him to think he had deprived her of so much when she had preferred to marry him rather than a wealthy and important Duke.

"I am afraid, my dear, the only thing we can afford is tea on the lawn, or perhaps a few people for supper in the Vicarage," he had replied.

Lady Louise laughed.

"Whom could we invite?" she asked. "You know most of the so-called Gentry around here have 'one foot in the grave', and all the young men in their families gravitate as soon as they are old enough to London, away from the quiet of the country."

"That is what we want," Daniel Forde said fiercely.

He had taken his wife in his arms and kissed her.

"I love you!" he declared. "Is that not enough?"

"It is all I have ever wanted, and what I have!" Lady Louise had answered softly. "But I was talking about Ula, darling, and not me."

"We shall just have to pray that something turns up," Daniel Forde said optimistically.

He had then kissed his wife again so that there was no chance of her saying any more.

It was after her father and mother's Funeral that Ula's Uncle had taken her back to Chessington Hall.

He was grumbling all the time what an expense she would be, and how the last thing he wished to do was to revive the memories of her mother's disgraceful behaviour by letting her meet his friends.

"Surely, Uncle Lionel, you are glad Mama was so happy?"

"If she was, she had no right to be," her Uncle replied harshly. "She behaved abominably, and although Avon married subsequently, I am sure he had never forgiven her for insulting him in such an outrageous fashion."

It was something Ula was to hear over and over again in the months to come.

Although it hurt her like the stab of a knife every time she heard her mother decried, it was impossible for her to answer her Uncle or defy him without being beaten for doing so.

The first time he struck her she could hardly believe it was really happening.

Her father had never in his whole life raised his hand to her, and even when she was a child, had never punished her, except by speaking to her severely.

Then, when her Uncle continued to beat her on every occasion he could find an excuse to do so, she realised it was because he was still infuriated that he could not call the Duke of Avon his brother-in-law.

It was also a humiliation that his sister had caused such a scandal.

On the other hand, Ula knew that the Countess disliked

62

her because she resembled her mother.

Although she had produced such an exceptionally beautiful daughter, the Countess herself was a plain woman.

The beauty in the family came from Lady Louise's mother who had been not only a famous beauty, but a woman of great charm and goodness who was the daughter of the Marquis of Hull.

Sarah was always told that she resembled her grandmother, and Ula, having seen portraits of the Countess, knew this was true.

Her own looks were, however, different from Sarah's.

Although she resembled her grandmother in her colouring, she had her father's eyes and, while she was unaware of it, his character which was exceptional.

Daniel Forde had talked to his daughter since she was very small as though she was grown up and could understand exactly what he was saying.

His philosophy of life, his kindness, his understanding of other people, had therefore been transmitted to her.

She had not only inherited this as his child.

He had also communicated to her the wisdom of his experience and made her aware, as he was, that everyone met in the world was a human being like oneself.

Ula had therefore grown up perceptively aware of other people's inner selves in a manner that was exceptional for a girl of her age.

She had known, as no one else would have, the reason why she had been treated so hatefully and cruelly at Chessington Hall.

Even though she understood it, it did not make the pain of it any easier to bear.

Night after night she had cried despairingly into her pillow, telling her father and mother how unhappy she was and finding it unbearable that they should have left her alone.

She was living with people who both condemned and

punished her for sins that she herself had not committed.

"Save me . . Papa . . save . . me!" she had cried the night before the Marquis had called on Lady Sarah.

When driven beyond endurance by Sarah's blows, by her Uncle's threats, and the fact that she was given so many services to perform and was punished when she was slow at carrying them all out, she had run away.

It was then that her father, by sending the Marquis to rescue her, had answered her prayers.

Every night since she had come to London she had thanked him on her knees and again before she had gone to sleep.

"How could I doubt Papa would save me?" she asked herself every morning.

She was sure when she put on the party gown which the Duchess had bought for her that her mother was looking at her approvingly from the other world where one day she would join her.

"I am so happy, so very, very happy! I feel it cannot be true!" she told herself on Friday morning.

By the time she had seen the Ball-Room decorated with garlands of flowers, with pink candles instead of white in the sconces and chandeliers, which the next day would be the talk of London, she was saying it again.

How could any girl not be happy when she had the most beautiful gown to wear she had ever imagined even in her dreams?

Then the Marquis had a new idea, which again would give the gossips something to talk about.

He had erected a small fountain in the Anteroom in the Ball-Room which sprayed, instead of water, a delectable perfume of roses.

"How clever of you to think of it, Drogo," the Duchess said.

"I must be honest and say that I saw something very like it in Paris when I was in the Army of Occupation," the Marquis replied. "But I think mine is an improvement

64

because the fountain in Paris sprayed champagne."

"I think scent is far more suitable for a *débutante*," the Duchess agreed.

To Ula it was the most fascinating toy she had ever imagined.

She realised the Marquis had exercised all his ingenuity to make the Ball different from any other Ball that had taken place recently in London, especially in regard to the decorations.

Not only were the candles pink, but the flowers were all pink and white, and the Chefs had been instructed to see that the supper echoed the same colours.

Up the stairway which led to the Ball-Room there were great banks of pink and white flowers.

The Marquis had arranged that at midnight pink and white balloons should be released from the top of the house.

They would float down into the garden where Chinese lanterns hung from the trees and the paths around the lawn and amongst the flowerbeds were picked out with fairy-lights.

It was all so beautiful that Ula was quite certain that no one would look at her.

But the gown the Duchess had ordered for her was as unusual and sensational as was everything else.

Because it was correct that she should wear white, her gown was white, but with a difference.

Underneath it there was silver sheath which fitted close to her body.

There was a fringe of *diamanté* falling around the hem, and from the exquisitely cut bodice which revealed the curves of her figure and set off the translucent whiteness of her skin.

Every time she moved she shimmered and glittered almost like a fountain, and there were diamonds sprinkled in her fair hair and on the shoes which peeped from beneath the hem of her gown.

She looked like a nymph that had risen from the lake and was still shimmering from the silver water.

"You look very beautiful, my child," the Duchess said as they met when she came into the Drawing-Room where the guests dining in the house were to assemble.

Ula watched to see if the Marquis approved, and she saw his eyes under his drooping eyelids flickering over her.

He himself was looking positively regal, wearing the Order of the Garter, and decorations on his evening-coat which had been awarded not only for his position at Court, but had also been won for gallantry in battle.

The diamond Garter around his leg and his exquisitely tied cravat would have made him outstanding even apart from his handsome looks, dark hair and broad shoulders.

"You look magnificent!" Ula exclaimed impulsively.

"You should be waiting to receive my compliments," the Marquis drawled with a bored expression on his face. "That is the way a young lady of fashion and, of course, an 'Incomparable' would behave."

For a moment Ula, thinking he was serious, looked upset and the colour rose in her cheeks.

Then she realised he was teasing her and said:

"Lady of fashion or not, I am speaking the truth, and I am sure that most of our guests, and especially the ladies like myself, would far rather look at you than at me!"

The Marquis laughed as if he could not help it. Then he said:

"Tonight it is you we are concerned with. You have to shine and make certain that everybody is aware of you."

"Now you are frightening me," Ula said. "Suppose I fail you, and you are angry?"

"If I am, I can always drown you in the fountain!"

She laughed again.

"That would be a delightful death, and certainly a very original one."

"You are not to talk of death," the Duchess said sharply, "it is unlucky. Tonight we are all very much alive, and remember, Ula, to enjoy your compliments and not be embarrassed by them."

"I shall not be embarrassed," Ula replied, "just suspicious that they are not sincere."

"They will be," the Duchess said firmly. "You can be sure of that!"

Ula certainly did receive a great number of compliments as soon as the guests began to arrive.

She was aware, too, that they looked at her with curiosity.

They also found it exceedingly surprising that the Marquis should have broken his rule of the past of never giving a Ball at his own house.

It was always thought, she had discovered, that it was something he would never do because he disliked people trampling about on his carpets and intruding into what he thought of as a private part of his life.

By the time dinner was ended and the Ball had started she found it impossible to think about anything except how thrilling it was to be part of it all.

As she was receiving by the side of the Marquis and the Duchess, it was quite obvious to everybody that the Ball was being given for her and she would undoubtedly be the talk of the men who came from the Clubs in St James's.

It was when about half the guests invited after dinner had arrived that, standing beside the Duchess and the Marquis, Ula was aware of who was coming up the stairs directly behind those who were just being presented.

There was no mistaking her Uncle's rather pugnacious face and the scowl between his eyes which she knew meant that he was very annoyed.

Nor could she miss the expression of anger in her Aunt's face, and when she looked at Sarah she realised how furious she was.

The Duchess greeted them first.

"How delightful to see you both," she said in her soft

voice, holding out her hand first to the Countess and then to the Earl.

"It is a long time since we have had the pleasure," he said somewhat grudgingly.

"We must talk about the old days later on," the Duchess said graciously.

The Earl passed the Marquis while the Countess lingered behind to talk to the Duchess.

"Nice to see you, Chessington-Crewe!" the Marquis said genially.

"I missed you the other day when you called on me," the Earl replied. "What happened?"

"Oh, something of no consequence," the Marquis replied in an unconcerned manner. "We must talk about it another time."

It was then the Earl moved to face Ula.

One moment he looked hard at her, and he looked so furious that she instinctively took a step back as if she was afraid he was going to strike her.

Then without saying a word he walked on.

The Countess reached the Marquis a moment later and then faced Ula.

She almost gasped as she took in Ula's appearance: the expensive and unusual gown she was wearing, the elegance of the way her hair was dressed. And her eyes did not miss the necklace of real pearls which the Duchess had lent her.

She looked her up and down as though she was a creature which she found singularly unpleasant, and then as her husband had done she walked on without speaking.

Lady Sarah halted in front of the Marquis.

"I have missed you," she said in a low voice.

Her face turned up to his was so beautiful that Ula could not imagine how any man could resist such loveliness.

"I am delighted that you were able to come tonight," the Marquis said in a noncommittal voice.

He would have turned to the next guest had not Lady Sarah held on to his hand.

"When shall I see you?" she asked.

"Later this evening, I hope," he replied.

It was not the answer she wanted, but he firmly removed his hand from hers to hold it out to the next guest who had already greeted the Duchess.

There was nothing Lady Sarah could do but move on another step and this brought her in front of Ula.

The expression on her face changed completely, and she was no longer beautiful, but almost ugly in her fury.

"I will kill you for this!" she hissed in a voice that only Ula could hear.

Then she walked on.

Chapter Four

The band was soft and melodious, the Ball-Room looked entrancing with its pink candles.

As Ula was besieged by would-be partners asking to be introduced to her, she thought everything was exactly as she had dreamed it would be, only even more marvellous.

She was, however, although she tried to suppress it, acutely conscious of her Uncle's and Aunt's and Sarah's hatred, which seemed to vibrate at her across the room.

She tried not to look in their direction, but when she did so she was thankful to find that Sarah was surrounded by young men, so that she could not complain on that account.

Nevertheless she knew, although it was ungrateful to think so, that they spoilt the party for her.

But she enjoyed every dance, only being disappointed that the Marquis did not ask her to dance with him.

However he had made it very clear before the Ball that he never danced if he could possibly help it.

"Sometimes it has to happen in the line of duty," he had drawled, "but I prefer cards, and that is where I shall be, if I have the chance."

Nevertheless Ula was aware that he was a conscientious and charming host, and there was no chance at all of his being relieved of his duties after the Prince Regent had arrived.

When Ula was presented to him, and sank down in a deep curtsy, she only wished that her mother could see her and know that at last she had attained all that she had longed for but had thought impossible.

"I am told you are a new beauty," the Prince Regent said in his thick voice, but with a smile that was irresistible.

"I am afraid, Sire, that your informants were being over-optimistic," Ula replied.

The Prince Regent thought this amusing and laughed.

"Are you really so modest?" he asked. "And you must not lie to me, for you look like a small angel who would always tell the truth."

"That is what I thought myself, Sire," the Marquis, who was standing beside him, remarked.

"If once again, Drogo, you have beaten me to the post," the Prince Regent said, "I shall be extremely annoyed!"

As if she thought he was being serious, Ula said quickly:

"I am sure, Sire, no one could do that, when Your Royal Highness's original ideas in the world of Art are known all over the country."

As the Prince was having difficulty in making even his friends appreciate his purchase of the Dutch pictures and some sculpture which had not yet become fashionable, he was delighted.

"I can see, Miss Forde," he said, "that I shall have to invite you to Carlton House to see my new acquisitions, and I can only hope that you will find them, if not superior to, at least different from what Raventhorpe has already packed into his 'Palace of Treasures'."

Ula laughed, knowing that the Prince, while he was genuinely fond of the Marquis, was also a little jealous of him.

"I hope, Sire," she said, "that is a promise you will not forget."

"I assure you I shall not do that," the Prince Regent said gallantly.

As he moved away to speak to somebody else, Ula glanced at the Marquis and knew from the expression on his face that he was pleased with her.

She felt a little thrill of delight that she had not failed in

71

what she knew had been a demanding test.

Then she saw the fury in the eyes of her Uncle, who was looking at her from the other side of the room, and it was like a douche of cold water drowning her feeling of pleasure.

She hurried back to the side of the Duchess.

"Here you are, child," she said as Ula moved close to her, as if she felt in need of protection. "I was wondering where you were because His Highness Prince Hasin of Kubaric is anxious to meet you."

Ula knew at once of whom the Duchess was speaking because the Marquis had in fact expressed extreme annoyance when the Turkish Ambassador had asked whether he could bring His Highness to the Ball.

"There are more than enough people as it is," the Marquis said when he received the Ambassador's letter, "but I suppose it is impossible for me to refuse him."

"I think it would make things very uncomfortable if you did," the Duchess replied. "I expect the Prince is staying at the Turkish Embassy, and there is nothing the Ambassador, who is really a very nice man, can do but get him invited to every entertainment that London provides."

With a somewhat bad grace the Marquis therefore sent a note to the Turkish Ambassador to say most untruthfully that he would welcome Prince Hasin to the Ball.

Since her father had been very interested in the different States in the East, Ula actually knew without being told where Kubaric was.

It was a small, so-called Independent, State where the Eastern Ottoman Empire bordered Afghanistan.

It had, she recalled, a great potentiality for the production of jewels, which lay mostly unmined in its mountains.

The reigning Prince, her father had told her, lived in great style while the mass of his subjects were miserably poor.

She therefore looked with interest at Prince Hasin as the Duchess presented her.

She saw that he was a man rising forty, slightly stout from what she was sure was soft living, and his face, which when he was younger could have been good-looking, showed signs of debauchery.

She suspected, amongst other things, that he indulged in the use of drugs which was so prevalent, her father had told her, in that part of the world.

When the Prince's eyes met hers, she knew that he was not only unpleasant but, in some way she could not define, dangerous.

She was sure of this when, as he took her hand and she sank in a low curtsy, she felt his vibrations were, if not evil, certainly extremely unpleasant.

She wanted to walk away from him immediately, but without being rude it was impossible for her to do so when he put his arm around her waist and drew her on to the dance-floor.

The Band was playing a Waltz which had just been introduced into England by the Russian Ambassador's wife, the witty Princesse de Lieven.

It was, however, frowned upon, being thought too intimate by a number of the older and more severe hostessses.

There was nothing Ula could do but let the Prince move her around the dance-floor to the strains of the romantic music.

She was uncomfortably aware that he was holding her closer than any of her other partners had done, and that his voice as he talked to her was deep with an emotion she did not like to define, even to herself.

"You are very beautiful, Miss Forde!"

Ula did not answer and he went on:

"Are you cold and reserved as so many English women profess to be, or is there fire behind those sparkling eyes, a fire which I wish to burn for me?"

With an effort Ula managed to say:

"I find it . . difficult to follow what Your Highness is . . saying when I am afraid of . . missing a step. I have not often . . danced the Waltz before."

"If I am the first to dance a Waltz with you," the Prince said again in that deep, rather frightening voice, "then I would wish to be the first to kiss you, the first man to awaken you to the joys of love."

Ula held herself as stiffly as she could and made no attempt to answer what the Prince had just said.

After a moment he remarked:

"I am told that your Uncle is the Earl of Chessington-Crewe, whom I have met on the Race-Course."

This, Ula thought, was safer ground and she quickly asked:

"Does Your Highness own race-horses?"

"Not in this country, but I am building up a stable in Kubaric."

"How interesting!" Ula said.

"I would like to show you my horses," the Prince replied, "and many other things as well."

Again there was something alarming in the way he spoke, but to Ula's relief the music came to an end and he was forced to follow her as she moved quickly towards the Duchess.

When she reached the Dowager, who was talking to several elderly gentlemen, Ula curtsied and said:

"I thank Your Highness."

"You will dance with me again."

It was a statement rather than a question.

"I am afraid that will be impossible," Ula said quickly. "Your Highness will realise that as the Ball is given in my honour my programme is already full."

There was an expression in his half-closed eyes which made her feel embarrassed and increased her dislike of him even more.

"I shall not forget you, Miss Forde," he said, and taking the hand she held out to him raised it to his lips.

Because Ula was wearing attractive mittens of fine lace

74

rather than gloves, she could feel his lips, thick, warm and sensuous on her skin.

She felt herself, as if touched by a reptile, shiver with revulsion.

Then after what seemed a long time he released her and to her relief she found the Marquis was at her side.

"Why were you dancing with the Prince?" he asked sharply in a voice that only she could hear.

"I . . I could not . . help it," she answered, "but . . please do not let him come . . near me . . again. There is something horrible about him which . . frightens me!"

She looked up at the Marquis as she spoke and saw an expression of anger in his eyes.

"That creature should not have come here in the first place," he said. "He is certainly not the sort of man with whom you should associate."

Then, before he could say anything, her partner for the next dance, a young man in the Household Cavalry, came to her side.

As they danced the Quadrille it was a relief to know that she need not be held close in the arms of a man she had disliked on sight.

At the same time for the rest of the evening she was aware that the Prince was watching her.

It made her feel self-conscious and as if she could not escape from his scrutiny any more than she could from her Uncle's, her Aunt's and Sarah's.

The Ball did not end until three in the morning when, despite protests from the guests who wished to go on dancing, the Marquis ordered the Band to play the National Anthem.

"It was such a wonderful party, how can we bear it to come to an end?" a very lovely lady glittering with a profusion of rubies in her dark hair said to the Marquis.

"You may not need your beauty-sleep, Georgina," the Marquis replied, "but my grandmother is growing old, and late nights are bad for her."

The lady called Georgina pouted her lips provocatively.

The way she looked at the Marquis told Ula that she was enamoured of him.

In fact she was only one of the many beautiful women she had noticed who all the evening had been fawning on him, putting their hands on his arm and lifting their lovely faces to his with what appeared to be an invitation in their eyes.

'And is it surprising that they find him irrestistible, when he is so handsome, and also so very kind?' Ula thought.

"A wonderful party, Drogo!" the Duchess said when the last guest had gone and she moved slowly across the hall towards the staircase.

"You are not too tired?" the Marquis asked.

"I am very tired," the Duchess replied, "but elated by the huge success that Ula enjoyed. Everybody, with the exception of three of our guests, told me how beautiful she was, and your men-friends all averred that she eclipsed any Beauty they had ever seen."

"I really cannot believe that," Ula protested. "At the same time, I am so glad that after all the trouble you have taken I did not let you down."

She was looking at the Marquis as she spoke, then added almost as if she wished to make sure:

"You . . you were not . . disappointed?"

"No, of course not," he said quite sincerely. "You were exactly what I wanted."

She knew he was thinking of the frustrated expression on her Cousin Sarah's face when she had said good night to him.

Ula was standing near enough to her to hear Sarah say:

"I am very hurt that you left the Hall after you had called the other day without seeing me."

"It was what I heard, rather than saw, which made me leave," the Marquis replied.

For a moment Lady Sarah did not understand.

76

Until as if she guessed the meaning of the words, she stiffened and there was a puzzled expression of concern on her beautiful face.

Then she turned away and went quickly away to join her father and mother who were just leaving the Ball-Room.

Ula went to bed feeling as if the dance-music was still playing in her heart, and the beauty of the scene was still floating in front of her eyes.

Because she only wanted to think of happy things, she deliberately forced herself not to remember the hostility of her Aunt and Uncle and Sarah.

She thought instead of the flattering things that her partners had said to her, and most of all the approval in the Marquis's eyes.

Then just before she fell asleep she remembered how much she disliked Prince Hasin and felt herself shiver.

Although the Duchess and Ula slept late, the Marquis was up early and as usual went riding in the Park.

He met a number of his friends and they all combined to tell him that the Ball he had given last night was the best they could ever remember, and it would be impossible for anyone else to rival, let alone eclipse it.

"You are very flattering," the Marquis said.

"I cannot think how you do it, Raventhorpe," one of the gentlemen on horseback remarked, "and it is no use our trying to beat you when you produce for our delectation an angel who only for you would have dropped out of the sky!"

There was a roar of laughter at this. Then somebody else said: "The Prince Regent always hits the nail on the head. Miss Forde does look exactly like an angel, and the proper place for her would be a shrine in your Hall at Raven where we can all light pink candles in front of her!"

There was more laughter, but as the gentlemen rode off the Marquis was thinking with satisfaction that it was he who had first thought Ula looked like an angel when he had given her a lift in his Phaeton to help her escape from Chessington Hall.

He, like Ula, had been well aware last night that the Earl and Countess had been furious at Ula's success.

They had found it difficult to realise that the radiantly beautiful girl who attracted everybody's attention was the wretched child they had ill-treated to the point where she could bear their cruelty no longer.

He was sure they were wondering how he had met her and by what supernatural means she had been transformed overnight into being the most talked-of and admired young woman in the whole of the *beau monde*.

The Marquis congratulated himself, feeling he had pulled off a coup that was even more satisfactory than winning a Classic race.

He had known it was with the greatest difficulty that the Earl had refrained from asking him searching questions as to how he had met Ula.

Sarah's obvious frustration because he did not go near her during the whole evening had pleased him as much as if he had won a large sum of money at the card-tables.

One look at her petulant face, when she was not deliberately smiling with what he was sure was an effort, told him he had had a very lucky escape.

Never would he endanger his freedom and risk his comfortable way of living by marrying anybody.

There were cousins who would succeed to the Marquisate, and if he did not have a son, why should that worry him after he was dead?

"I will never marry," he vowed, "and never again will I be fool enough to be deceived by a woman!"

The cynical lines on his face were even more deeply pronounced than usual as he rode back to Berkeley Square.

He found, as he expected, that he was to breakfast alone, there being no sign of either of the ladies.

He was quite content, but he would have been even more

pleased with himself if he had known of the scene that was taking place two streets away.

It was in the imposing residence the Earl had bought, gambling on his daughter being the outstanding success she had undoubtedly been up until last night.

The Earl had come down to breakfast first in a bad mood.

He had drunk too much of the Marquis's excellent champagne and even more of his superb claret, with the result that his right foot in which he suffered from gout was paining him.

He was helping himself to a dish of sweetbreads and fresh mushrooms when to his surprise his daughter Sarah joined him.

"You are very early, my dear!" he remarked.

"I could not sleep, Papa, how could I?"

Sarah certainly looked very pale, the Earl thought.

With her hair hanging down her back and wearing an unattractive robe in which she usually rested in the afternoons, she did not look as beautiful as usual.

"You should have slept until luncheon-time," he said gruffly.

"How can I sleep when I can only think about the way Ula was disporting herself last night? And how she can afford a gown which must have cost far more than any gown you have ever bought me!"

Her voice rose a little shrilly and the Earl replied:

"I suppose all those rumours we heard about her being chaperoned by the Duchess because she knew her mother are true? Anyway, we will be able to find out more."

"How when she ran away did she get to the Duchess?" Sarah asked. "Unless, and this is a possibility, Papa, the Marquis took her there."

She sat down at the table as she went on:

"If you think that was what happened, she must have appealed to him somehow to take her away in his Phaeton, and that was why he left."

"If you remember," the Earl said heavily, "the footmen said, and there is no reason why they should lie, that he walked out of the Anteroom while you were in the Drawing-Room, and went straight to the stables."

As the Earl spoke Sarah sat bolt upright in her chair.

"Did you say the servants said he came out of the Anteroom?"

"That is what Henry told me," the Earl replied, "and I see no reason why the boy, stupid though he is, should not tell the truth."

"I distinctly gave instructions to Newman that the Marquis should be put in the Library until I was ready to see him," Sarah said.

She thought for a moment, then went on:

"Olive and I were talking in the Drawing-Room. You do not suppose, Papa, that if the Marquis was in the Anteroom he overheard what we said?"

"Was there any reason why your conversation should upset him?"

"Every reason!" Sarah gasped.

Then she gave a little scream.

"I am sure now that is why he left. Oh, my God, Papa, you will have to do something! You will have to prevent him from puffing up Ula, which is what he is doing just to punish me!"

"I do not know what you are talking about," her father protested.

"But I do!" Sarah went on. "I do not believe for a moment the story that the Duchess of Wrexham loved Aunt Louise so much that she wanted to help her daughter."

She screamed the next words:

'It is the Marquis who is at the bottom of this! The Marquis who is having his revenge on me!"

"If that is true," said the Earl, who was finding it difficult to follow his daughter's train of thought, "I will wring your neck for losing the richest and most important son-in-law I am ever likely to acquire!"

"I will not have Ula taking my place as the most beautiful girl in England!" Sarah cried. "I will not have her wearing better gowns than I possess, and having a better Ball than you ever gave me, with every man who has hitherto admired me, now admiring her!"

Her voice rose again to a scream as she went on:

"I will not have it, Papa! Do you hear me? I will not have it!"

Then as the Earl stared at her, as if he was not quite certain what all the commotion was about, Sarah burst into tears.

The Duchess and Ula had luncheon alone together.

"I thought it would be a mistake after such a late party, dear child, for us to accept any of the many invitations we had for today," the Duchess said.

"You are quite right," Ula agreed, "and I think, Ma'am, you ought to rest this afternoon."

"And what will you do?"

"I shall read a book," Ula replied. "When I first saw His Lordship's Library I knew there were at least two or three hundred books I wanted to read, and the sooner I get started, the better!"

The Duchess laughed.

"You are far too lovely, my dear, for there to be any need for you to be a 'Bluestocking'."

"I have no wish to be that," Ula said. "At the same time, Papa always said a pretty face is a good introduction, but a man wants something more if he is to enjoy the company of one woman for the rest of his life."

"So you are talking about marriage," the Duchess smiled. "How many proposals did you receive last night?"

"You will hardly believe it," Ula said, "and I feel quite certain by this morning they will have changed their minds,

81

but there were no fewer than three young men who said they intended to ask if they could pay their addresses to me."

The Duchess laughed.

"It is what I expected."

"I cannot believe it possible," Ula said, "that any man could imagine he wants to marry a woman with whom he has danced only once!"

"Most women do not look like you, my dear," the Duchess said, "and I am sure the men in question were all frightened that somebody else might steal a march on them by getting there first."

Ula was silent for a moment. Then she said:

"It is strange . . but each one began by saying: 'Are you in love?' When I shook my head they said: 'Then if you are not in love with the noble Marquis, I have a chance.' "

The Duchess smiled, then she said insistently:

"I do beg of you, my dear, not to fall in love with Drogo."

Ula's eyes opened wider than usual as she said:

"Why do you think that I should presume to do anything so foolish?"

"Because inevitably women want what they cannot have," the Duchess replied. "So many women have done everything in their power to get Drogo to give them the quite inexpensive, but inexpressibly valuable present of a gold ring."

She looked at Ula, then said as if she wanted to impress it upon her:

"I am quite sure that the very unpleasant experience my grandson has had with your Cousin Sarah will make him revert to what has been his intention ever since he was quite young, and that is never to be married."

"But, of course," Ula said, "he is quite right, unless he really falls in love with someone. I am sorry Sarah should have hurt him and perhaps made him very cynical, but I know he would have been very unhappy with her."

"I am aware of that now," the Duchess said. "Like many

other men, Drogo was for a time blinded by her beauty."

She sighed before she said almost to herself:

"But she is the only girl, and this is unfortunately the truth, whom he had ever seriously considered making his wife, and I think it will be a long time before he recovers from the blow inflicted upon him."

"I can understand that," Ula said in her soft voice, "but as Papa often said, 'time heals many things'. Although the Marquis is now bitter and upset, I am sure he is such a marvellous person that he will find somebody to love, and love is the quickest healer of all."

The Duchess smiled.

"Only you could think like that, my child, and what we have to do is to find you a husband you love and who does not love you just for your pretty face."

Ula was silent, and the Duchess knew she was remembering how much her mother had loved her father and he her.

She found herself praying that the child would not be disappointed or disillusioned as her grandson had been.

She was sure, even from the few days she had been with her, that Ula was very vulnerable and very sensitive.

'She must find the right sort of man,' the Duchess thought, 'a man who will protect her and keep her from anything that could spoil her intrinsic purity and goodness.'

Then she was surprised that she could apply such words to someone who being so young would obviously still be quite immature.

She was well aware however that Ula was different from most girls of her age, for her character and personality were unusually developed for her years.

"In fact she is exceptional," the Duchess told herself.

She had already made up her mind that, when the Marquis had finished using her as a tool to enact his revenge on Lady Sarah, she would look after her at her house in Hampstead, and try to find her a husband who would make her really happy.

After the Duchess had gone up to rest, saying they had only a small dinner-party to attend that night and so would be able to get to bed long before midnight, Ula went into the Library.

As she had said, there were so many books she wanted to read that she did not know where to begin.

She had just found one that looked particularly interesting because it was about horses, when the door opened and the Butler announced:

"His Highness Prince Hasin of Kubaric to see you, Miss!"

Ula started and almost dropped the book she was carrying.

The Prince came into the room looking more bombastic than he had last night.

His dark eyes as they appraised her in the daylight seemed even more embarrassing than they had under the crystal chandeliers with their pink candles.

"I am delighted to find you alone," the Prince said as the servant shut the door behind him.

He advanced across the room until he reached her side.

Ula curtsied, then she said quickly:

"I am afraid, Your Highness, that as Her Grace has retired to rest being somewhat tired after last night, it is incorrect for me to receive visitors in her absence."

"You will receive me," the Prince replied, "because I am here, and because, my beautiful Miss Forde, I want to talk to you."

Ula held the book she was carrying tightly against her breast, almost as if it protected her, as she said:

"I regret, Your Highness . . that is . . impossible!"

"That word is not in my vocabulary," the Prince said.

He moved a step nearer as he said:

"Let me look at you. You are even lovelier today than you were last night, and having found you, my precious pearl, I have no intention of losing you."

"I would . . not wish to . . insult Your Highness," Ula said in a voice that shook a little, "but if you will not . . leave . . me then I must . . leave you."

She moved away from him as she spoke, but he reached out and caught her by the wrist.

"Do you really think I will allow you to leave me?" he asked in an amused tone of voice. "I find you entrancing, even when you are resisting me, and because you are so small and at the same time so lovely, I cannot fail to teach you to obey my commands."

"Please . . do not . . touch me!" Ula said, trying to free her wrist from his clasp.

But he merely pulled her closer to him.

Then he unexpectedly put out his other hand and taking the book from her flung it down on the floor.

She realised as he did so that he intended to draw her closer still and kiss her.

With a little cry of horror she tried to struggle against him, frantically attempting to release his grip on her wrist.

Then as she did so he gave a low laugh that was little more than a sound which came from between his lips, and she knew perceptively that because she was trying to escape, because she was fighting against him, it only amused and excited him all the more.

"Let me . . go . . please . . let me . . go!"

Her voice was low and frightened.

"That is something I have no intention of doing," the Prince replied.

Relentlessly he drew her nearer and nearer to him with what seemed an iron grip.

She gave a little scream as his other arm went around her.

Then as he bent his head towards her lips she screamed again, and as she did so the door opened.

For one second she could hardly believe she was saved, but standing staring at the Prince and looking extremely angry was the Marquis.

It was then that his grip relaxed and Ula with a swift movement was able to free herself.

She ran across the room to fling herself against the Marquis and hide her face against his shoulder.

He did not put an arm around her, but he felt her whole body trembling against his.

Then to her surprise the Marquis said in a cold, hard, and at the same time controlled voice:

"I think Your Highness must be unaware that my grandmother, being old, is finding it impossible to receive visitors today after the festivities of last night."

The Prince did not speak, but as he looked at the Marquis it was as if the two men challenged each other.

"You will therefore understand," the Marquis continued, "that you were admitted by mistake, and I can only ask Your Highness if you will be so gracious as to call on another occasion."

"I came to see Miss Forde," the Prince said at length.

To Ula it was if he snarled the words as an animal might have done.

"I think Your Highness must be unaware," the Marquis went on in the same cold and lofty tone he had used before, "that in England young women of gentle birth do not receive gentlemen alone without a chaperon being present."

The Prince was beaten and he knew it, but he managed to give a somewhat forced laugh as he said:

"English traditions! English protocol! So very difficult for those of us who come from other countries."

"Exactly!" The Marquis replied. "I knew Your Highness would be intelligent enough to understand."

He reached out to pull the door a little wider open, and although the Prince tried to bluster his way towards it, there was no doubt it was a humiliation.

Deliberately the Marquis, without turning Ula around, moved her to one side, and following the Prince into the passage he said:

"Your Highness must allow me to show you to your carriage."

He shut the door behind him and Ula, as she sank down in a chair, heard them walking down the passage towards the hall.

She was still trembling and feeling as if she had passed through a terrifying experience and had been saved from utter destruction only by the intervention of the Marquis.

She hated the Prince and feared him in a way she had never been afraid of anyone before, not even her Uncle, in the whole of her life.

She was sure he was evil, she was sure he personified everything that was debauched and wicked.

And yet she had no valid reason for thinking this, only an instinct that made her still tremble at the thought of his kissing her.

The Marquis came back into the room.

"How can you have been such a little fool . . " he began.

Then he saw Ula's face looking up at him, his anger seemed to evaporate and he said:

"I realise you did not expect him. That is the truth, is it not?"

"I had . . no idea he . . would call on me," Ula answered. "I . . I hated him last night . . when I had to dance with him . . and if you had not saved me . . he would have . . kissed me!"

The terror in her voice was obvious.

The Marquis walked to stand with his back to the mantelpiece.

"Forget him," he said. "I should have been sensible enough to refuse the Turkish Ambassador's request that he should be included among my guests last night.

"I shall now give instructions to the servants that if he ever comes here again they are to say that no one is at home."

"Thank . . you," Ula whispered.

Then after a moment, as if she had thought it over, she said:

"It was . . stupid of me to have . . been so . . frightened, but I did not . . know there were . . men like him in the world."

"There are unfortunately quite a number of them," the Marquis said coldly, "and you have to learn to take care of yourself."

"I . . I will try," Ula said humbly, "but I cannot help thinking I . . might have encountered somebody like him . . rather than you . . when I . . ran away."

"Prince Hasin is not the sort of man you will meet as a general rule in anyone's house, unless you are particularly unfortunate," the Marquis said. "I know his reputation, and once again I can only say that I made a mistake in allowing him to come to the Ball last night."

"It was such a wonderful Ball," Ula said in a soft, quiet voice.

"You enjoyed it?"

"More than I can ever tell you. It is something I shall always remember."

"I hope it taught your Uncle and your Cousin a lesson they will never forget."

There was a note in his voice which made Ula say involuntarily:

"No . . please . . do not speak . . like that!"

"Why not?" the Marquis asked.

"Because it . . spoils you."

He looked at her in astonishment and she explained:

"You will think it very . . presumptuous and perhaps very . . impertinent of me . . but you are so magnificent in . . yourself, so kind and so wonderful, that it . . spoils you when you are . . vindictive . . and too petty to be . . worthy of what you . . really are."

She spoke hesitatingly, stumbling a little over the words. Then she said quickly:

"I . . I am not putting it very well . . but it is what I feel is . . true."

The Marquis looked at her for a long moment, then he walked to stand at the window looking out into the garden.

The gardeners and a number of servants were busy removing the Chinese lanterns from the trees and lifting up the fairy-lights which had edged the paths.

He did not see them. He was looking back into the past when he knew he had in fact been a very different person from what he was at the moment.

Then he had been young and idealistic, and had believed, as his mother had taught him, that in his position he had to set an example of everything that was fine and noble to those who served and looked up to him.

He wondered now if he had lost that ideal, when behind him he heard a very small voice ask:

'You . you are not . . angry with . . me?"

He turned around.

Ula was looking at him somewhat piteously, and he knew she was afraid of what she had just said.

"I am not angry," he said quietly, "and I have an uncomfortable feeling that you are right."

Chapter Five

Ula awoke with a feeling of happiness.

She had gone to bed after a quiet dinner with the Duchess and the Marquis, and they had laughed a great deal as they talked over everything that had happened the night before.

There were lots of things to amuse them.

One of the guests had held a wineglass under the fountain spraying perfume and said:

"I am sure this wine is delicious!"

Then as he took a large gulp from the glass, he had not known whether to spit it out or swallow it!

There were some very amusing incidents in the garden when, trying to catch the balloons that were floating down from the top of the house, several ladies and gentlemen had fallen into the flower-beds, and a woman's gown had been set on fire by one of the fairy-lights.

It was very quickly extinguished, and only scorched a frill on her gown, but she screamed and made as much noise as if she had been burned at the stake.

They also laughed over the many compliments the Marquis had received.

The Duchess had found many of her friends with *débutante* daughters had tried to be congratulatory about the magnificence of the Ball, but found it difficult.

When dinner was over the Duchess said:

"I have never enjoyed your company more, Drogo, or known you in better form, but now unfortunately as I am so old I must go to bed."

"Of course you must rest," the Marquis said, "for I believe there is another Ball tomorrow night at which Ula must consolidate her position as a great beauty."

"I am quite certain she will do that," the Duchess said, patting Ula's arm affectionately.

"Will you be accompanying us?"

"It is unlikely," the Marquis replied, "as I shall not return to London until late in the evening."

"Where are you going?" the Duchess asked.

"To Epsom," the Marquis replied. "Have you forgotten there is racing there tomorrow?"

"Oh, of course," the Duchess replied, "and I suppose as usual you will win all the important races."

"I sincerely hope so," the Marquis replied.

"I wish I could come with you!" Ula exclaimed impulsively.

The Marquis looked at her, then he said:

"I never thought of it, but of course another time I will take you racing, especially when I am sure my horses are going to win."

"That will be wonderful!" she exclaimed.

But as they walked out of the Dining-Room she had the feeling that tomorrow he would be accompanied by one of the beautiful women who had been at his side last night.

It was nothing he had said, and yet she was sure it was the truth, and somehow she felt suddenly lost and alone as if no one really wanted her.

"So you will not be in to dinner tomorrow?" the Duchess was saying as they moved along the passage.

"No," the Marquis replied, "I am dining with the Cavendishes, so if I do not turn up at the Ball you will realise the dinner finished too late for me to appear."

"I understand," the Duchess said, "and Ula and I must not complain, for you have been very generous in dining with us tonight. I suppose, unlike us, you do not intend to go to bed early."

"I promised His Royal Highness I would look in at Carlton House," the Marquis replied, "and after that I have several other invitations."

He spoke slightly mockingly and again Ula was certain the invitations came from lovely women who would be waiting anxiously for him.

She went up the stairs with the Duchess who on reaching her room said:

"Good night, my child. My grandson is delighted with the successes of last night and how beautiful you looked."

"Does he . . really think . . that?" Ula asked a little wistfully.

"He told me this morning that you exceeded all his expectations."

She saw the light that came into Ula's eyes and the sudden radiance on her face.

She did not say anything, but merely kissed the Duchess good night and went into her own room.

"I do not want the child to break her heart over Drogo," the Duchess murmured to herself, "but what can I do about it?"

When she got into bed and her maid had turned out the lights she did not sleep at once, but lay worrying over the two young people who filled her life at that particular moment.

Ula had gone to bed with the Duchess's words ringing in her ears, and she thought that nothing else mattered if the Marquis was really pleased with her.

'I must be very, very careful,' she thought, 'to do everything he wants, and not make any mistakes.'

When she said her prayers she thanked God that the Marquis had come in time to save her from Prince Hasin, and she added a little plea that she need never see the Prince again.

She had been told not to hurry up in the morning but to rest while she had the chance.

She therefore had her breakfast in bed and was not ready

to go downstairs until it was nearly eleven o'clock.

It was a luxury she had never known to be waited on and be able to do exactly what she wanted.

All the last twelve months at Chessington Hall she had been expected to be down as early as the servants, knowing that there were a dozen tedious jobs waiting for her which she had been unable to finish the night before.

She put on one of the pretty morning-gowns which the Duchess had bought for her.

This particular one, which was a very pale blue like the sky in the early morning and trimmed with broderie anglaise threaded through with matching velvet ribbon, was not only very pretty but also very smart.

As she went downstairs she took with her an attractive shawl in case when she went out into the garden the sun was not as warm as it looked.

She felt it was unlikely to be necessary and she therefore when she reached the bottom of the stairs put it on a chair in the hall.

Then she went as if drawn by a magnet into the Library, hoping that today she would not be interrupted in her desire to read as she had been yesterday.

Because she thought it reminded her of the Prince, she did not take from the shelf the book he had snatched from her arms and thrown on to the floor.

She chose another one, this time a book of poems by Lord Byron.

She had only just settled herself comfortably in the window-seat and started to read one of her favourite poems when the door opened and the Butler announced in a rather strange voice:

"The Earl of Chessington-Crewe, Miss!"

For a moment Ula was frightened into immobility.

Then as she looked across the room at her Uncle coming through the doorway she saw that following him was a Bow Street Runner.

She thought her eyes must be deceiving her, but there

was no mistaking his red coat and his official hat which he carried in his hand.

As the Earl reached the centre of the Library he stood still and said in a voice of command:

"Come here, Ula!"

Because she was so frightened she rose a little unsteadily to her feet and walked very slowly towards him.

When she reached him he looked down at her with an expression on his face which she knew was one of contempt before he said:

"I have come to take you back to where you belong and we are leaving immediately!"

"But . . Uncle Lionel . . I cannot do . . that!" Ula cried. "I am staying here . . as you know . . at the invitation of the Duchess of Wrexham, who is . . chaperoning me."

"I am aware of that," the Earl replied, "but you appear to have forgotten when you ran away in that disgraceful manner, for which you shall be severely punished, that now your father and mother are dead I am your Guardian."

"I . . I know that, Uncle Lionel, but you . . did not . . want me."

"That is for me to say," the Earl replied. "Now, I have no time to waste in arguing, so you will come with me, and my carriage is outside."

He spoke so positively that Ula gave a cry of fear.

"I . . cannot! I have to . . stay here, and if you want me to . . leave you must discuss it . . with the . . Marquis."

"As I have already said," the Earl replied, "I am your Guardian, and if you intend, as I suspected you might, to oppose me, I have brought with me, as you can see, a Bow Street Runner."

There was a sneer on his face as he continued:

"He will take you into custody and you will appear before the Magistrates. They will tell you that as a minor you will have to obey me. That is the law."

He paused as if he expected Ula to reply.

Her voice seemed to have died in her throat and she could only stare at him in a stricken manner.

"If that is what you prefer," he said slowly and spitefully, "then at the same time, when they make it clear to you that I have complete and absolute control over you, I will bring a charge against the most noble Marquis of Raventhorpe of kidnapping a minor – the penalty for which is transportation."

He spoke spitefully, knowing that after what he had said there was nothing she could do but agree to go with him.

Then as if he wanted to humiliate her he said sharply:

"Well – what is your decision?"

"I . . I will come . . with you . . Uncle Lionel."

"Then hurry up about it," he ordered.

He took her by the arm, holding her so tightly that it was painful, and marched her from the Library, along the passage and into the hall.

The servants waiting there stared at them in astonishment, and as they neared the front-door Ula with an effort managed to say:

'Please . . Uncle Lionel, I must say . . good-bye to . . Her Grace and fetch my . . bonnet and shawl."

"There is no need for you to make any farewells," the Earl replied, "and I can see a shawl on the chair."

He pointed towards it and one of the footmen who had been staring was galvanised into picking it up and bringing it to Ula.

She put it around her shoulders and to enable her to do so, her Uncle took his hand from her arm.

As he did so Ula made an effort to dash away from him and up the stairs.

He however had anticipated that was what she might do, and he struck her sharply across the shoulders causing her to give a little scream of pain and to stagger.

However she regained her balance and did not actually fall on to the floor.

Then the Earl took hold of her once more, and dragging

95

her through the front-door and down the steps he almost hurled her into the travelling-carriage that was waiting for her.

He paused briefly to pay the Bow Street Runner before he entered the carriage, the door was shut and the horses started off.

Ula had a quick glimpse of the servants clustered on the doorstep to watch her go.

But as she sank back on the seat making herself as small as possible, she knew she was leaving behind the place that had been a Heaven of happiness and returning, as she had told the Marquis, to what was undoubtedly Hell.

Feeling she must make one more desperate plea, she said to the Earl:

"Please . . Uncle Lionel . . listen to me . . I cannot . . "

"Be quiet!" he thundered. "I have no wish to talk to you until we reach the Hall when you will be punished for your appalling behaviour. After that I will tell you what I have planned for your future. Until then, be silent!"

He roared the last words at her, then putting his feet up on the seat opposite he leaned back and shut his eyes.

Ula looked at him and wondered how it was possible that anyone so cruel and callous could be her mother's brother.

Yet frightened as she was, she knew there was nothing she could do but pray that by some miracle she would be saved.

Not only from the beating that her Uncle obviously intended to give her when they reached Chessington Hall, but also from the way of life that had been so unendurable that she had run away.

"Save me . . Mama . . save me!"

Then instead of seeing her mother's face as she usually did when she prayed, she saw the Marquis's. He had saved her once. Could he do so again?

She felt her whole being crying out to him, telling him of her plight.

96

Then she remembered that he would be away for the whole day, first racing, then dining with his friends.

She was certain the party included some beautiful lady who would amuse him so that he would never give her a thought or have any idea what was happening in his absence.

She remembered he had said he was dining with the Cavendishes, and it was then she recalled that the beautiful lady festooned with rubies whom he had addressed as Georgina was the wife of Lord Cavendish.

As she felt agonisingly that it would be a long time before he learned what had happened to her, she knew that she loved him.

It was not a shock, but she knew that ever since he had appeared like a Knight coming to her rescue, he had filled her with thoughts of her dreams to the exclusion of everything else.

'Of course I love him!' she thought. 'How could I do otherwise, when he is so handsome . . so magnificent . .- and so different from . . any other man?'

Because she had been worshipping him as her Saviour, she had not thought of him as being in the same category as the men who had paid her extravagant compliments, or who incredibly had wanted to propose marriage.

She knew now why it had simply never occurred to her as possible that she might love them, or in fact any other man.

Her whole being vibrated to the Marquis and he seemed, like the sky, to overshadow everybody else until they shrank into insignificance.

'I love him! I love him!' she thought as the horses, by now on the country roads, moved more and more quickly.

'I love him . . although he will never know it, and no other man can ever mean anything to me, however long I may live.'

Suddenly the idea came to her that if she had to escape again from the intolerable treatment she would receive at Chessington Hall, doubtless worse than it had been before, the only thing she could do would be to die.

"Then I will be with Mama and Papa," she told herself.

At the same time, she now knew she would be reluctant to leave the world behind because the Marquis was in it.

It took them nearly two hours to reach Chessington Hall, and all the time she forced herself to think only of the Marquis.

Somehow it gave her the courage to step out of the carriage after her Uncle with her chin held high.

She knew the servants whom she had come to know so well were staring at her as she walked up the steps looking very different from the way they had last seen her.

"Good day, M'Lord!" Newman the Butler said respectfully as the Earl strode into the hall and one of the footmen took his hat.

There was no reply from the Earl and Newman smiled at Ula as he said:

"Nice to see you again, Miss!"

She gave him a piteous glance and before she could speak the Earl roared:

"You will come with me, Ula!"

He walked as he spoke towards his Study and she knew with a sudden constriction of her heart that he was going to beat her with the long, thin riding-whip which cut the delicate skin of her body like a knife.

She wanted to scream, she wanted to run away, but because she knew it was useless and at the same time she wanted to behave with the courage the Marquis would expect her to show, she just followed her Uncle.

He walked into the large Study in which he habitually sat, its dark velvet curtains seeming to exclude the sunlight even when they were drawn back.

He stood in front of the mantelpiece as Ula stood just inside the door, as if waiting for his command.

"Now that I have brought you back to where you belong," he said, speaking as if he was addressing a large audience, "I will tell you what I have planned for you, after you have been punished for running away and putting me to a great deal of trouble."

"I . . I am sorry to . . upset you . . Uncle Lionel," Ula said, "but I was so . . unhappy that I could not . . bear it any longer."

"What do you mean, unhappy?" the Earl roared, "and why should you expect happiness? You, an orphan whom I was charitable enough to take into my house when you were left homeless and penniless by your ne'er-do-well father!"

It was the kind of abuse which Ula had had to endure for a year, but she merely drew in her breath and forced herself not to reply.

"After which you have the effrontery," the Earl went on, "to revive the old scandal that I hoped had been forgotten of your mother's appalling behaviour in running away and disgracing the whole family."

His voice rose as he said:

"You are no better than she was, and yet despite your ingratitude, I have, and it is a great deal more than you deserve, arranged your marriage, which will take place immediately."

Ula stared at her Uncle in sheer astonishment.

"Arranged . . my marriage . . Uncle Lionel?"

"God knows why anyone should want to marry you!" the Earl declared. "But I am thankful, indeed very grateful, that you will be off my hands and, which pleases me even more, out of this country, so I need never see you again."

"I . . I do not . . understand," Ula said.

"Then let me tell you of your good fortune," her Uncle replied. "His Highness Prince Hasin of Kubaric has asked for your hand in marriage!"

Ula gave a scream that seemed to echo around the walls of the Study.

"Prince Hasin?" she gasped. "It cannot be true . . and I will not marry him . . nothing in the . . world would make me . . marry him!"

She moved towards her Uncle as she spoke saying:

"He is horrible . . repulsive . . and I would rather . . die than be his . . wife!"

"How dare you speak to me like that!" the Earl roared. "You should go down on your knees and thank God that any man, considering your background, would marry you!"

"I will not do it . . I will not!" Ula cried. "I hate him . . don't you understand? He is . . loathsome!"

She thought her Uncle would shout at her louder than he had already. Instead he reached out and hit her hard on the side of the head.

She was not expecting it and she fell down, bumping her head as she did so against the leg of the chair.

For the moment there was nothing but darkness.

Ula slowly came back to consciousness to hear Sarah's voice:

"What has happened, Papa? I see you have brought Ula back, but why is she lying on the floor?"

"I suppose she has fainted," the Earl admitted grudgingly. "I will bring her round."

Ula heard him walk across the room as he did so and knew he was going to the grog-tray that stood in one corner.

"She looks very pale," Sarah said.

"I will pour this water over her," the Earl said. "She will soon come round."

Sarah gave a shriek.

"No, Papa, no! You will spoil her gown, and as it is far smarter than anything I own and far more expensive, I want it for myself. I am sure it will only need lengthening."

Ula did not move. She was feeling weak and her head ached, and she had no wish to face her Uncle or Sarah.

She heard her Uncle put down the jug of water on a side-table before he said:

"Damn the girl! She is nothing but a nuisance!"

"I hope, Papa, you are going to beat her for the way she has behaved," Sarah said in a spiteful voice.

"I have every intention of doing so," the Earl replied, "but the Prince will be here with the Special Licence which he is obtaining from the Archbishop of Canterbury."

"I do not think it right that Ula should be a Princess," Sarah complained.

"She can call herself anything she likes as long as she stays in Kubaric," the Earl said. "I do not expect she will much enjoy herself there with three other wives waiting to scratch her eyes out!"

Ula drew in her breath and realised in horror that what he had just said implied that the Prince was a Muslim.

In which case he was entitled to four wives and she would only be one of them.

For a moment she could hardly believe that any man could call himself a Christian and at the same time consign her to such a fate.

Then she knew that the Earl would accept anything or anybody so long as she was taken away from England and out of his sight.

Almost as if what she was thinking gave Sarah the same idea, her Cousin said:

"Well, we need not worry about her once she is gone. Did you see the Marquis when you collected her from his house?"

"No, of course not," the Earl replied. "I knew that Raventhorpe was at Epsom where he has several horses running."

"That was clever of you, Papa, and if the Prince marries Ula tomorrow morning, it will then be too late for him to interfere."

"Do you really think he will try to do that?" the Earl asked.

"He has only set her up as a beauty because he is angry with me," Sarah replied. "Once she is out of the way I will get him back."

"I hope you are right," the Earl said dryly. "You cannot 'play fast and loose' with a man like Raventhorpe."

Sarah was not listening.

"I want that gown, Papa," she said.

Ula was aware that she was looking down at her.

"Have her taken upstairs and undressed. After that you can beat her until she is dead, for all I care!"

"It would be a mistake to upset Prince Hasin," the Earl said. "He wants some horses to take back with him to Kubaric, and I have some which I intend to show him tomorrow before the marriage takes place."

"Well, all I want is Ula's gown," Sarah said, "although if His Highness throws in a few diamonds, I shall not say 'No'!"

"Leave everything to me," the Earl replied.

A voice from the door interrupted them.

"You rang, M'Lord?"

"Yes, Newman," the Earl replied. "Have Miss Forde carried upstairs, undressed and put to bed."

"Very good, M'Lord."

"She is not to be taken into her old room," the Earl went on, "but somewhere where she has no clothes. She must be rendered unable to escape. Do you understand?"

"Yes, M'Lord."

"Put her in the Oak Room at the end of the passage of the first floor and tell the housemaids when they have undressed her that Lady Sarah wants her gown. Miss Forde is to be locked in the room and the key brought to me. Is that clear?"

"Yes, M'Lord."

"If she escapes again," the Earl continued, "anyone who helps her or lets her go will be dismissed immediately and without a reference!"

"I understand, M'Lord."

Ula heard Newman step back and he must have beckoned to one of the footmen.

A few moments later someone lifted her shoulders,

someone else her feet, and she was carried from the Study, through the hall and with some difficulty up the stairs.

The whole household must have been aware by now, Ula thought, that something unusual was happening.

She could hear the housemaids chattering at the top of the stairs before the men carrying her reached them.

"Miss Forde is to go in the Oak Room at the end of the passage," Newman said.

He repeated the Earl's instructions about removing her gown and locking her in, and that if anyone helped her escape they would be instantly dismissed.

"Her's fainted," one of the women said as the men put her down on the bed.

"I heard His Lordship knock her down," Newman replied, "and she must 'ave hit her head against something."

"Oh, poor young lady! 'T'isn't fair!"

Ula knew it was Amy who spoke. She was one of the younger housemaids and a very nice girl.

"Now, you be careful, Amy," Newman warned. "If Miss Ula runs off again, we'll be in the soup."

"If you asks me, Mr Newman, it's a cryin' shame the way His Lordship treats her, an' I've always said as much."

"Then you keep your ideas to yourself," Newman answered, "or you'll find yourself crying outside the back-door! Come on, James."

The two men left the room as he spoke, and Amy and the other housemaids undressed Ula.

She was determined to remain, as they thought, unconscious, and she made herself completely limp as they took off the beautiful gown which Sarah coveted.

Then having fetched it from her bedroom upstairs, they dressed her in one of her old, worn and darned nightgowns.

Ula lay stiffly without moving until the housemaids had left, and she heard the key turn in the lock.

Only then did she open her eyes and look around her frantically, wondering if there was any means of escape.

She knew however that unless she had wings and could fly it would be impossible to get out by the window.

The house had been built with high Georgian ceilings and even from the first floor, if she fell from a window on to the gravel below, she would certainly break at least a leg or her back, even if she did not kill herself.

She sat up in bed looking at the large mahogany wardrobe, the dressing-table, the wash hand stand with its china ewer and basin, the chairs and other smaller pieces which furnished the room.

It was very much better than the room she had been given originally which was really a servant's room on the second floor.

At the same time she was aware that the wardrobe was empty.

Although she could see that the housemaids had besides her nightgown brought down a plain flannel dressing-gown she had worn for some years and a pair of slippers, there was nothing else in which, if she wanted to, she could escape.

"What can I do? What . . can I do?" she asked in a whisper.

Once again she was sending out a frantic winged prayer to the Marquis, pleading with him to come to her rescue.

She knew it was impossible, and yet he had saved her before when she was running away from Chessington Hall without even a penny in her pocket in an effort to get to London.

He had saved her once already from Prince Hasin, and perhaps, by a miracle, he would do so again.

Something she decided during the long hours in which no one came near her was that she would rather die before she allowed the Prince to touch her, although she had no idea how she could do so.

There were, she knew, guns in the gun-room and sharp knives in the kitchen, but they were all inaccessible.

Half a mile from the house, if she could get there, there

was a swift-moving stream, and she thought that in certain parts of it the water would be deep enough for her to drown.

But with the door locked there was little or nothing she could do about it.

"Help me . . God, please . . help me. There must . . be a way. There must be some manner of . . escape before I am to . . marry the Prince!"

Having studied Eastern religions with her father, she knew it was very easy for a Muslim to divorce any wife with whom he was bored.

If the Prince already had three wives, which was more than likely, because in the East the men started marrying when they were very young, he only had to say: 'I divorce you', and he was free to marry another woman.

But it was not so much being the wife of a Muslim that appalled her, but the thought of belonging to the Prince.

The evil she had immediately felt in him seemed in her imagination to be all around her.

She wanted to scream and go on screaming so that she could somehow express her terror and her horror of what awaited her.

At five o'clock in the evening Ula heard someone outside the door, and as the key turned in the lock she quickly lay down and shut her eyes.

She did not need to be told it was her Uncle who had come into the room, and she sensed, although she did not look at him, that he had come to beat her as he intended.

When he came up to the bed she felt he was surprised at finding her as he thought still unconscious.

She knew he was looking down at her, because she could hear him breathing heavily as if it had been an effort to walk up the stairs.

She did not move and after a moment he said:

"Ula! Wake up! Do you hear me? Wake up!"

There was a note of authority in his voice which made it

difficult for her not to obey him.

Then as if he was anxious because she appeared to be unaware of what was being said, he bent forward to take her by the shoulders and shake her.

He shook her backwards and forwards, but with an effort of willpower which came from her fear of being beaten, Ula forced herself to be limp under his hands.

She let her head fall backwards and forwards as if she had no control over it.

Then with an oath beneath his breath her Uncle threw her back against the pillows.

As he did so Sarah came into the room.

"Ula cannot still be fainting, Papa!"

"I think she must have a touch of concussion," the Earl said slowly, as if it was difficult for him to admit it.

"Well, she had better come round before tomorrow, if that is when she is to be married."

Her father did not reply and Sarah went on:

"Mama says I am to lend her one of my gowns or give her back the one in which she arrived, but I have something white which I do not want and it will be quite good enough for her."

"The Prince can certainly afford to buy her anything she wants," the Earl said.

"Then she is lucky!" Sarah sneered. "I could do with quite a lot of things!"

"If the Prince buys my horses at the high price I intend to ask for them," the Earl said, "you shall have a new gown as soon as we get back to London."

"Then let that be the day after tomorrow," Sarah replied, "or better still, tomorrow afternoon. I want to see the Marquis, and now that Ula is out of the way he will soon be back in my pocket – you see if I am not right, Papa."

"I hope you know what you are talking about," the Earl said, "but come on, we can do no good here."

Ula heard him stride out of the room and Sarah followed him, then once again the key was turned in the lock.

She got out of bed and walked once again to the window.

Was it possible, she wondered, to make a rope with the sheets from the bed?

She had nothing with which to cut them, and she knew that tied together even with the blankets they would not be nearly long enough to reach the ground.

"Help me! Please, God . . please . . Papa . . help me!"

There was nothing she could do but pray and now she thought of how cleverly her mother had escaped the night before her marriage.

No one had been aware of it until the next morning when it was far too late to find her.

She and the man she loved had already been married in a small country village by a Parson they had got out of bed to see the Special Licence they showed him.

She felt herself shiver at the thought that a Special Licence was what the Prince was getting now.

She knew they would be married in the village Church where the Vicar, who was an old man, had been appointed by her Uncle.

Even therefore if she protested at the altar that she had no wish to be married, it was doubtful if he would listen to her.

She went on praying until the sun was sinking behind the trees in the Park and the shadows had grown very long.

Then, unexpectedly, she heard the key turn once again in the lock, and before she had time to get back into the bed the door opened.

To her relief it was not her Uncle as she feared, but Amy, the young housemaid who had come to the Hall at about the same time as she arrived.

She came into the room.

"Are you better, Miss Ula?" she asked. "We've been ever so worried about you."

"I am worried about myself," Ula replied.

"I 'ears you're to be married tomorrow. Do you feel well 'nough?"

"It is not a question of feeling well," Ula answered. "Prince Hasin is an evil, wicked man and I simply cannot marry him."

Amy looked at her in surprise. Then she said:

"I can understand you not wantin' to marry a foreigner! At th' same time, you'll be a Princess!"

"Yes, Amy," she said, "but I shall not be properly married as you understand it. Prince Hasin is a Muslim, and is allowed by his religion to take four wives.'

"Four wives, Miss? I've never 'eard of such a thing!"

"I know that my father, who was a Parson, would be horrified at the idea, and my Uncle the Earl is only allowing the Prince to marry me because he wants me out of the way."

"You're too pretty, Miss, that's the whole trouble. It's that Lady Sarah. They say she's been jealous ever since you first comes 'ere."

"Yes, I know. Amy, but what matters now is that I have to get away somehow, as I did before."

"There's no way you can do that, Miss. If I 'elped you, as I'd like to do, I'd only be dismissed without a reference, and these days jobs be 'ard to come by."

"I understand," Ula said, "but Amy, I am hungry."

"I was thinkin' about that, Miss, an' 'Is Lordship said you was only to 'ave dry bread and water, but Cook's ever so sorry for you – we all are – an' after they've gone in to dinner I'll bring you somethin' nice to eat an' a cup o' cocoa."

"I would like that, Amy. Thank you very much."

"I'd best go now, Miss, in case 'Is Lordship sees.

Amy smiled at her, slipped out of the room and turned the key in the lock.

Ula sat looking at the closed door.

Then she had an idea.

Chapter Six

It was after half-past eight when Amy came back with Ula's dinner.

By this time she was really hungry, despite the fact that she was so frightened that she thought the food might choke her.

At the same time she had eaten nothing since breakfast in London.

She lay in the dark thinking about the Marquis, and when Amy came in to light the candles and pull the curtains she felt almost as if he was inspiring her to find a way of salvation.

The plate of fish that Amy had brought upstairs was delicious, and she watched with satisfaction as Ula ate nearly all of it.

Then when she had drunk a little of the cocoa Ula said:

"I am going to ask you to help me, Amy."

"You knows I'd do anything you ask me, Miss, but I can't let you escape, an' your room with your clothes in it has been locked an' His Lordship asked for th' key."

Ula thought her Uncle was taking every precaution to prevent her from escaping. Then she said:

"Sit down, Amy, and I will tell you my idea."

A little apprehensively Amy sat down on the edge of a chair looking at Ula with worried eyes.

"I have got to get away from here," Ula said. "If I cannot escape, then I shall have to kill myself, and that is not an idle threat."

"You can't do that, Miss, it'd be real wicked!"

"I know, Amy, and my father would be very upset if he knew. At the same time, I cannot marry Prince Hasin."

Even to think of him made her temble, but she forced herself to go on.

"What I want to do, Amy, if you are brave enough, is to come back here when the others have gone to bed and say, if anybody asks you, that you had forgotten to collect my tray."

She saw Amy was listening so continued:

"Your story tomorrow will be that I overpowered you, tied you up, and escaped before you could prevent me or call for help."

She looked at Amy who was staring at her wide-eyed, and she went on:

"One thing I promise, that is if my Uncle does turn you out, which I think in the circumstances will be unlikely, you can go the Duchess of Wrexham or to the Marquis of Raventhorpe, and I am certain because they are fond of me that they will give you a position the same as you have here."

"You're sure o' that, Miss?"

"Quite sure," Ula replied. "Frankly, my only alternative would be to throw myself out of the window, but I do not think I would be killed, only maimed, perhaps for life."

Amy gave a cry of horror.

"I can't let you do that, can I? But, Miss, I'm afeared for you an' for meself."

"I know, Amy, that I am asking a great deal of you," Ula answered, "but you are literally the only person I can turn to for help."

Her voice was pleading, and after a moment, as if she could not help herself, Amy said:

"I'll help you, Miss. It's not right you should be treated that badly by His Lordship."

"Thank you," Ula said simply. "There is nothing I can give you to show how grateful I am, but I feel that one day you will be rewarded for being so brave."

"It'll be in Heaven, if His Lordship guesses the truth!" Amy said with a flash of humour.

"If you are clever, His Lordship will think that I over-powered you when you least expected it. After all, you are not very big, and he would believe anything of me as long as it was bad enough."

There was a little pause, then Amy said:

"Will you tell me, Miss, what you wants me to do?"

"I want you to come up before His Lordship goes to bed, but when it is late enough for the other servants not to notice you have disappeared."

"I understands, Miss," Amy said. "I'd better go now."

She stood nervously looking over her shoulder as if she half-suspected that somebody was listening to their conversation.

She peeped out of the door, then hurried away locking Ula in as she had before.

It was an hour and a half before she returned, and as she turned the key, Ula watching the door was frightened in case instead of Amy it would be her Uncle.

But Amy came in quickly and shut the door behind her saying as she did so:

"I tells 'em down below I were a-comin' to bed, an' they paid no attention."

"Where is His Lordship?" Ula asked.

"He be sitting in the Study, and Mr Newman said he were 'drunk as a Lord' afore he left the Dining-Room."

Ula thought that was encouraging and Amy went on:

"Mr Newman says Lady Sarah were going on at him to beat you as he says he would, but he tells her you had to be well enough to be married as soon as the Prince arrives."

Ula did not wish to hear any more.

"Now listen, Amy, I want you to lie down on the bed as you will be tomorrow morning when they find you."

Amy did as was suggested and raised her head so that Ula could tie a napkin which had come up with her dinner over her mouth and knot it at the back.

Then she pulled it down on to her neck and said:

"It will not be uncomfortable, for you need not adjust it until just when you think you might be discovered and are shouting for help."

"When'll that be, Miss?"

"As late as you can. The longer they assume I am here and not you, the more chance I have of getting away."

Amy seemed to understand this and then Ula showed her how to tie her ankles together with the silk cord which had held back the long curtains over the window.

"You can put that on easily," she said, "but now, this is the one difficult part."

She had taken a soft linen face towel from the wash hand basin and twisted it so that it made two holes into which Amy could easily slip her hands.

Then when she pulled her hands apart the knots tightened so that it appeared as if she could not move.

"If you put your hands close together," Ula explained, "you can easily release yourself so as to be able to tie your legs and put what is meant to be a gag over your mouth."

She went on speaking slowly so that Amy would understand.

"Then at the last moment, you slip your hands into the towel and lie down, saying you have been in that position all night."

She did not say so to Amy, but she thought that when it was discovered she had run away, there would be so much consternation over her disappearance that they would pay no particular attention to the way in which the maid was tied.

Ula made Amy rehearse what she must do several times before she was quite certain she understood. Then she said:

"Now I am going to leave, but, Amy, I shall take the key so that when they hear you screaming they will have to break down the door."

"'Is Lordship said as 'ow he wanted the key with 'im tonight,' Amy replied.

"When he finds it is not there, he will think you have gone to bed and taken it with you," Ula said, "and if, as Newman says, he has drunk a great deal of claret and port, he will not worry about that until the morning."

She had known for some time that the Earl was accustomed to drink heavily when he was worried about anything or was angry.

In fact always before he beat her she knew that he had drunk several glasses of wine or brandy.

This inflamed his feelings so that she thought he was often more brutal than he really intended to be.

Before Amy came back Ula had put on her dressing-gown which was made of very pale blue wool.

It buttoned down the front and had a small collar edged with narrow lace.

Her mother had made it for her many years ago, and although it still fitted her, it was rather short.

But she had nothing else to wear and she was only thankful that when the housemaids had fetched her night-gown from her bedroom they had brought down her bedroom slippers as well.

"I am going now, Amy," she said to the maid who was watching her with frightened eyes. "Pray, as you have never prayed before, that I may get away, and thank you, from the bottom of my heart, for helping me."

She kissed Amy gently as she spoke.

Then she opened the door and, going out into the passage, turned the key in the lock and started to hurry towards the back stairs.

By this time the maidservants, who all had to get up early, would have retired to the top floor where they slept in a small, low-ceilinged rooms.

The menservants slept downstairs and she knew they constituted a danger.

113

But there was no sound coming from the Pantry as she neared the bottom of the stairs, and she had no intention of using the back-door, but one which led into the garden.

It was locked and bolted for the night and she opened it as silently as she could, then stepped out into the fresh air.

The sun had sunk, darkness had come and the stars were still coming out in the sky while the moon which was only half full had just begun to rise above the trees.

Even without its light Ula could have found her way through the gardens and down into the Park.

She was wise enough not to run, but moved slowly, keeping in the shadow of the bushes, since because she was wearing a pale colour it would have been easy for anyone to see her.

Only when she was in the Park was she out of sight of the house and ran quickly into a small wood which led to open fields on the other side of it.

She realised that she must put the longest distance possible between herself and the Hall before grooms on horseback would be sent out to look for her as soon as it was discovered she had escaped.

There was also still the danger that the Earl might sense that something was wrong and insist on Amy being wakened so that he could have the key of the Oak Room door returned.

If Amy was found to be missing he would certainly be suspicious and the chase would begin, however late it might be.

"Help me, Papa . . please . . help me!" Ula prayed as she crossed the fields, walked through small copses of trees and found her soft bedroom slippers very inadequate protection for her bare feet.

The moonlight got brighter and now, even though it was easier to see her way, she was still terribly afraid of being noticed.

She tried to keep to the woods of which there were many,

but the pine-needles and the rough paths made it painful and difficult to hurry.

It was really easier in the fields.

Then at last, when she knew she had come a long way and was feeling very tired, she saw ahead of her a light which she could not understand.

It was in the middle of a wood through which it was difficult to move swiftly because of the dense undergrowth.

She thought perhaps it was a fire that had been lit by some woodcutters, in which case she must avoid them.

They would certainly think it very strange for a young woman to be roaming about alone late at night.

Then as she moved a little nearer, she saw with a leap in her heart it was not woodcutters who were in the open clearing, but Gypsies.

There were four painted caravans, and seated around the fire were the dark-haired Gypsy men and their brightly dressed women.

Without hesitating Ula moved towards them.

A man noticed her first and gave an exclamation. Then all the Gypsies turned to stare at her with their dark and, she thought, hostile eyes.

She went on until she stood beside them, before she said in Romany:

"Good evening, my friends!"

Now they looked at her in astonishment and a man said:

"Who are you, and how do you speak our language?"

"I am your blood sister," Ula said, and she held out her wrist on which there was a small white scar.

One of the Gypsies, who was a tall man, rose to his feet and she guessed he was the leader or father of the family.

He looked at Ula's wrist, then he spoke quickly in Romany to the others.

Ula knew he was telling them that what she said was true: she had exchanged her blood with a Gypsy and was therefore, as she had claimed, their sister.

Every year a tribe of Gypsies had camped in a field next to the Vicarage when they came to Worcestershire for the plum-picking.

Her father's Parish was in the very heart of the plum-picking district, and Ula had known and talked to the Gypsies ever since she was a small child.

It was typical that Daniel Forde should befriend the people who were scorned or feared by the rest of the community.

Those who did not accuse the Gypsies of thieving were afraid that they would cast an 'evil eye' on them or perhaps steal their children.

Ula's father had laughed at their fears.

"They are people without a land, and yet are a part of the English countryside. I have always found them completely honest except with regard to the wild animals and birds which they think God created for every man."

However, few people listened to him and the local land-owners refused to have Gypsies on their estates although they used them not only for the plum-picking, but also for getting in other crops for which they did not have enough local labour when the harvest was ready.

Ula had learnt a little Romany from the Gypsies.

Because they were so grateful for her father's and mother's kindness, when she was five years old and a son had been born to their Chief, and her father had christened the child, he said:

"There's little I can give you, Sir, in gratitude for your kindness to me and my people, but if you'll allow me, I'll make your daughter my son's sister by the joining of their blood. Wherever your daughter goes, she'll always be welcomed and helped by the Gypsies, and all that they own will be at her disposal."

Because he spoke with such sincerity, Daniel Forde knew it would have been an insult if he had refused the offer.

He had therefore allowed the Gypsy Chief to make a tiny cut on Ula's wrist and similarly on his son's.

Then as he held their two hands together and their blood mingled, he recited an incantation which had its origin in antiquity.

"Now I am a Gypsy, Mama!" Ula had said gleefully.

"You do not look like one, my darling," Lady Louise had laughed. "But who knows, one day you may need the Gypsies' help, though as things are they are far more likely to need ours."

Ula knew now that the Gypsies would help her, and it must have been her father who had answered her prayers and brought her to them.

She sat down by the fire and explained why she was running away because she was being forced into a marriage which was repulsive.

They seemed to understand, and when she asked them: "Where are you going?", she thought before they answered she might have guessed that once again her father had not failed her.

"We are going to Worcestershire," one of the Gypsies replied. "First there'll be the potato-lifting, after that the hop-picking, then the plums afore we move on."

"May I beg of you to take me with you?" Ula asked. "I warn you there may be enquiries about me, so I have to hide."

"You can hide in our caravans," one of the Gypsy women said, "and as Zokka's about the same size as you, she'll find you some clothes."

"Thank . . you . . thank . . you!"

Because Ula was so relieved and so very grateful, there were tears in her eyes and her voice broke on the words.

The Marquis returned to London very late because although he had told his grandmother he was dining with the Cavendishes he should not have used the plural.

It was Lady Georgina Cavendish who was waiting for him when he arrived at the large house that was not far from Epsom.

Lord Cavendish, as he had anticipated, was attending an important debate in the House of Lords.

The Marquis had enjoyed an excellent day's racing.

Two of his horses had come in first, and another which he was trying out for the first time had run extremely well and, although it was not placed, he had high hopes for its future.

Epsom was a small Race-Course, but he often thought it more enjoyable than the larger ones.

It was also convenient for London, and he knew when he finally returned home the roads would be clear, and as it was a moonlit night his superb horses would not make the journey tedious.

Lady Georgina was looking very attractive, not decorated with her famous rubies, but wearing a necklace of emeralds which seemed to be reflected in her eyes.

They slanted up a little at the corners which gave her a mysteriously feline expression, which the Marquis had found provocative and alluring ever since he had met her.

And yet tonight when finally he left her he thought, although it seemed incredible when she was so beautiful, that somehow she had proved disappointing.

She was certainly everything that any man might have desired from a passionate point of view.

Yet when he left her *Boudoir* and she clung to him, her warm body seeming to merge with his, he suddenly knew he was impatient to return to London.

"When shall I see you again, my wonderful lover?" she whispered in her low, seductive voice which many men had found irresistible.

"I am not certain of my plans," the Marquis replied evasively.

"I will let you know when next George is away," she said, "and anyway, I am coming to London the day after tomorrow for the Ball at Devonshire House."

She waited for him to say how much he would be looking forward to seeing her, but the Marquis was actually thinking that Ula would enjoy the Ball at one of the most attractive and important houses in London.

Georgina pressed herself a little closer and pulling the Marquis's head down to hers whispered:

"I love you! I love you, Drogo! If I do not see you again I shall die!"

This was an over-dramatic protestation which the Marquis had heard many times before and he merely said:

"You are far too young and beautiful to die, as you well know."

"I cannot live without you."

Now her voice was even more passionate than before, and the Marquis unlocked her clinging arms and kissed her lightly on the forehead.

"Go to bed, Georgina," he said, "and if you must dream of me, do not talk in your sleep."

Before she could prevent him he had pulled open the door, smiled at her, then was hurrying down the passage as if he was escaping from something which no longer interested him.

Georgina Cavendish walked back to the sofa to fling herself down once again on the soft satin cushions.

It was always the same, she thought: the Marquis left her before she was ready for him to go, and she had the frightened feeling that she might not see him again.

"I want him, oh, God, how much I want him!" she murmured.

Then she closed her eyes sensually as she remembered the sensations he had evoked in her.

The Marquis, however, as he drove his high-perched Phaeton along the main road towards London, was thinking that he was no longer interested in Georgina as he had been, and it would be a mistake to try to fan a dying fire.

He was accustomed to having his love-affairs come to an end, but usually not so completely as he knew unmistakably this one had done.

He could not explain it to himself, because Georgina was undoubtedly very beautiful, very sophisticated, and very experienced in the arts of love.

He found himself thinking of Ula's little flower-like face and of how much she resembled an angel – a description he certainly could not apply to the sensuous Georgina Cavendish.

He thought with satisfaction that as he would not be going to Epsom again for some time, he would not have to explain why he had not been to dine with her, and it would be far easier to avoid her in London.

Then he was thinking once again about Ula and remembering what a sensation she had caused at his Ball.

He was quite certain that by this time there would be a mountain of invitations waiting for her in Berkeley Square.

She would be the talk of the town while Sarah Chessington-Crewe was forced to take a back place.

He expected to feel elated at the thought, until he remembered how Ula had said that he spoiled himself by being vindictive.

"She is right – of course she is right," he said beneath his breath.

At the same time, it seemed to him extraordinary that a girl of her age should not only think such a thing, but be brave enough to say it.

He wished now he had left Georgina Cavendish directly after dinner so that he could have seen Ula before she went to bed.

But he knew that by the time he reached Berkeley Square she and the Duchess would have been in bed for hours and he would have to wait until the morning.

He drove his horses with a flourish up to the front-door of his house, certain that he had done the journey in record time and had once again proved that his horses were thereby superior to anybody else's.

Two grooms were waiting and as they ran to the horses'

heads the Marquis threw down the reins and climbing down from the Phaeton walked over the red carpet into the lighted hall.

It seemed to him there was unusual number of servants waiting for him considering it was so late, and then as Dalton hurried forward he realised that something was wrong.

"Thank goodness you're back, M'Lord!" the Butler exclaimed.

The Marquis, holding out his high hat to a footman, asked sharply:

"Why? What has happened?"

"I think, M'Lord, I should speak to Your Lordship privately."

The Marquis realised the footmen all had expressions of consternation on their faces, and he was also aware that the housemaids, very unusually at this time of night, were peering over the banisters on the second floor.

Because he knew it was a mistake to ask questions with the staff listening, he walked quickly towards the Library, and as Dalton followed him he asked sharply:

"What has occurred?"

"It's Miss Ula, M'Lord. She's been taken away!"

As the Butler spoke the Marquis felt as if it was something he might have anticipated, and he asked grimly:

"What has happened? Tell me exactly!"

"The Earl of Chessington-Crewe, M'Lord, arrived here soon after eleven o'clock with a Bow Street Runner."

"A Bow Street Runner?" the Marquis ejaculated. "What the devil did he come for?"

"I think, M'Lord . . ' Dalton began pompously, then went on, "in fact, M'Lord, I happened to overhear what His Lordship says to Miss Ula."

The Marquis knew this meant he had been deliberately listening, but he did not interrupt and Dalton went on:

"His Lordship informed Miss Ula that she was to return with him immediately and that if she refused to do so the

Bow Street Runner would take her before the Magistrates, where she would be informed that she had to obey her Guardian."

The Marquis made an inarticulate sound, while Dalton continued:

"He further informed Miss Ula, M'Lord, that if this happened, he would also bring a charge against Your Lordship for the abduction of a minor, the penalty for which he says is transportation."

"Good God!" the Marquis exclaimed furiously. "Are there no depths of iniquity to which that man will not descend?"

Dalton hesitated for a moment, then he said:

"There's something else, M'Lord."

"What is it?"

"While the Earl was in here with Miss Ula, M'Lord, the footman on his carriage who came with him from the country told Henry and John who were on duty in the hall that Miss Ula was to be married by Special Licence to a foreign Prince. They didn't catch his name, M'Lord."

For a moment the Marquis seemed speechless. Then he said:

"So that is what he is planning! I can hardly believe it!"

"The Earl's footman, M'Lord, seemed to think the marriage would take place tomorrow morning."

"That is something I shall definitely prevent."

"If you'll excuse me saying so, M'Lord,' Dalton said, "I can't help thinking that the foreign Prince is the gentleman who called the day after the Ball."

He paused before he continued:

"As I know the Butler who's working at the Turkish Embassy, in fact he's a distant relative of mine, I thinks I should warn Your Lordship that Prince Hasin's not a fit husband for any young woman, and especially anyone gentle and kind as Miss Ula."

"I am well aware of that," the Marquis said.

"My relative has told me tales of His Highness's behaviour," Dalton went on, "which are so unpleasant, so disgusting, that I would not soil my lips by repeating them to Your Lordship."

He looked at the Marquis almost pleadingly as he said:

"There's never been a young lady come to this house, M'Lord, who's been kinder or more pleasant to every one of us, including Willy whose finger she healed, and who thinks she's an angel sent from Heaven to help him."

The Marquis thought it was extraordinary how everyone high or low should react in the same way to one young woman, but he merely said:

"Will you order Crusader to be brought round from the stables in an hour's time. I want a drink, a bath, and I will change into my riding-clothes. The Phaeton is to follow me."

There was a smile on Dalton's lips as if this was what he wanted to hear as he hurried to obey his master.

The Marquis looked at the clock over the mantelpiece and reckoned he could reach Chessington Hall by about seven o'clock.

It was most unlikely that Ula's marriage would take place before that, and if he rode across-country he would have time to plan out exactly how he could save her from Prince Hasin.

When the Marquis was really angry, those who knew him well were aware that he became icily calm, and his voice seemed devoid of emotion, but had the sting of a whiplash.

As he now moved towards the door, not hurrying, but as if he had a sense of purpose which was more effective than speed, Dalton said:

"I begs Your Lordship's pardon, I forgets to say that Her Grace asked whatever time you returned, you'd go and see her."

"I will do that," the Marquis replied.

As he walked upstairs he knew he did not want to talk about Ula or what had happened, but to kill someone in her defence.

*

The Earl, because he was in a hurry for the next day to arrive, did not sleep well and rang earlier than usual for his valet.

He always rose at about seven o'clock, but this morning he was awake at six-thirty and before he left his bedroom he said to his valet:

"Fetch Mrs Newman to me. I wish to speak to her."

It was only a few minutes before Mrs Newman in her rustling black gown came hurrying along the passage.

"You wanted me, M'Lord?" she asked.

"Yes, Mrs Newman. See that Miss Ula is dressed in the white gown Lady Sarah has chosen for her, and she can have the use of the family wedding veil, which I know you have in your possession. But she is not to leave her bedroom until I send for her."

"I understand, M'Lord. Unfortunately there is a little – difficulty."

"What do you mean – a little difficulty?" the Earl asked in an irritated tone.

"Miss Ula's crying for help, but unfortunately we can't find the key of the room and I hears Your Lordship didn't take it with you last night when you retired."

The Earl thought for a moment before he replied:

"That is true. I told Hicks to bring it to me, but he said it was not in the door and he thought that – what is her name? – Amy must have taken it upstairs with her."

Mrs Newman paused for a moment before she said:

"Amy wasn't in her room, M'Lord, when the other housemaids rose at five o'clock, and they thought she must have gone downstairs early, but they've not found her."

"What the devil's going on?" the Earl said angrily.

"I've no idea, M'Lord."

"Then find out! Find out!" he said sharply. "And if you cannot find the key, then get somebody to break the lock."

As if he was suddenly aware that something untoward was happening, he walked quickly out down the corridor until he reached the Oak Room at the end of it.

There were two housemaids and the man who did odd jobs standing outside it looking puzzled.

They stepped to one side as the Earl approached the door and hammering on it with his fist shouted:

"Is that you, Ula?"

"Help! Help me! Please – help me!" a voice cried.

"What is happening?" the Earl demanded.

"Help! Help!"

He could hardly hear the voice which seemed somewhat muffled and turning to the servants he roared:

"Open this door immediately. You, Jacob – surely you can do something?"

"Someun's gone for t'carpenter, M'Lord."

This meant the estate carpenter who did not live in the house, and the Earl with a rising fury shouted:

"The whole house cannot be so full of nitwits that they cannot open a door! Tell Newman to bring the footmen upstairs."

It took nearly a quarter of an hour before finally somebody managed to break the lock.

By that time the Earl, shouting instructions and cursing everybody, was in such a rage that when everybody stood back for him to enter the room, he was almost incapable of doing so.

When he saw Amy lying on the bed, her wrists apparently tied together, and a silk cord around her ankles, he was for the moment speechless.

Then with a stream of oaths he began to berate her for allowing Ula to escape.

She burst into tears, and he hurried out of the room and down the stairs, shouting for Newman to send all the grooms to go in search of Ula immediately.

"She cannot have got far!" he stormed as he reached the hall.

Newman was waiting and he said in a quiet voice which was very much in contrast to the Earl's:

"Excuse me, M'Lord, but the Marquis of Raventhorpe

has called and I've shown His Lordship into the Study."

"The Marquis! He is at the bottom of this!" the Earl ejaculated, crossing the hall to fling open the door of the Study.

The Marquis, looking exceedingly elegant, his highly-polished riding-boots reflecting the sunlight coming through the window, was standing in front of the fireplace.

The Earl glared at him.

"What do you want?"

"I think you know the answer to that," the Marquis replied coldly.

"If you are after that damned niece of mine," the Earl said, "then you will have to find her. She has disappeared, and I suppose it is your doing! I will take you to the Courts over this, Raventhorpe."

"You can take me where you please," the Marquis said, "but am I to understand that you intend to marry Ula to Prince Hasin of Kubaric?"

"What I do is none of your damned business," the Earl replied. "She will marry the Prince if I have to thrash her insensible to make her do so!"

"I suppose you have some idea of the Prince's reputation?"

"I have no intention of discussing it!"

"Then I will tell you about him," the Marquis said without raising his voice and making every word seem to ring through the Study. "Prince Hasin is so steeped in vice that it is impossible to speak of his habits without being physically sick."

He then related quietly and calmly the varied erotic pleasures in which the Prince had indulged himself since he had been in London and which were obviously part of his life in his own country.

It was as if the Marquis hypnotised the Earl into listening, and when he had finished the Earl, as if he must assert himself, grew more crimson in the face than he was already.

"Even if what you say is true, which I very much doubt,"

he said, "I do not intend to go back on my word. His Highness has asked to marry Ula, and however important you may think you are, Raventhorpe, you cannot go against the law. As Ula's Guardian, I have given my promise to this marriage and there is nothing you can do to stop it."

"But you tell me that Ula is missing," the Marquis remarked.

"She will not go far, wearing nothing but a nightgown," the Earl replied. "My grooms are out on horseback looking for her, and when she returns she will marry the Prince within the next two hours."

"That is what I intend to prevent," the Marquis said, "and if it means rendering the Prince incapable of playing his part as a bridegroom, I shall not hesitate to do so."

"I will see you in jail for this, Raventhorpe!" the Earl shouted. "You are only a lecher who would not stoop to marry my niece with her scandalous background, and have doubtless taken advantage of her in a more convenient manner!"

He sneered the last words and the Marquis said coldly:

"If you were a younger man, I would knock you down for making such an infamous suggestion, but what I intend to do will, I think, prove more painful. I personally will make sure you are thrown out of every Club of which you are a member, starting with the Jockey Club and White's."

"You would not dare do such a thing!" the Earl retorted, but his eyes were wary.

"I consider you to be a man of no principles or decency, and therefore not fit to associate with a Gentleman!" the Marquis said. "I am not making idle threats, and it is something to which I will attend as soon as I return to London."

He walked across to the door as he added:

"In the meantime, as I have no wish to be in your company for one second longer than is necessary, I intend to go myself in search of Ula. When I have found her I shall take her back to the protection of my grandmother where she will remain while you consider what proceedings to take against me."

He paused before he said:

"Make no mistake, Chessington-Crewe, not only will I reveal from the witness-box your brutal treatment of a helpless orphan, but I will inform them in detail of the Prince's predilection for very young girls and children, in spite of which you consider him a suitable husband for her."

He paused to add in a voice like the crack of a whip:

"I shall find it strange after that if either you, your wife, or your daughter dare show your faces in London again."

The Marquis did not wait for an answer and left the room.

Only when he was alone did the Earl, as if he could no longer support himself, sink down into an armchair.

Chapter Seven

The Marquis walked into the Drawing-Room where his grandmother was sitting.

She looked up eagerly as he appeared but knew at once by the expression on his face that there was no news.

He walked slowly across the room as if he was very tired and sat down beside her.

She was silent and after a moment he said in a voice she had never heard from him before:

"What am I to do, Grandmama? I have looked everywhere! How could anyone disappear so completely? Unless of course she really was an angel and has gone back to where she came from!"

He thought as he spoke that must be the only explanation and that Ula was dead.

Every day since her disappearance he had ridden round the boundaries of the Earl's estate, occasionally encroaching into his woods when he thought it would not be noticed.

He was aware at the same time that the Earl's grooms were searching them very thoroughly.

He had also enquired of the people in the adjacent villages who assured him, he was convinced truthfully, that they had not seen her.

Eventually, when he thought he could bear it no longer, he employed divers to go down into the deep pools of the stream which passed over the Earl's land, increasing in size when it left it.

He had watched the divers and for one moment it

seemed almost as if he could feel a knife stab at his heart when he believed they had found her body.

One of the divers had come to the surface to say he had discovered something, he was not quite certain what it was.

When he went down again it turned out to be only the carcass of a sheep.

It was then, as he felt relief flood over him, that the Marquis admitted finally and irrevocably to himself that he loved Ula and could not contemplate life without her.

Although he had ridden until dark as he had done every day for nearly a week, he was still no wiser when he went home as to where she could be.

He experienced a feeling of utter despair he had never known before in his life, but he did not wish to upset his grandmother.

She had cried for two days after Ula was lost, as had most of the maids and other women of the household.

"Somebody must have hidden her," the Duchess said, "because otherwise she would have been very noticeable, wearing only her night attire."

It was something she had said hopefully over and over again, and the Marquis was trying to make some optimistic reply when the door opened and Dalton came in.

The Marquis looked at him enquiringly and he said:

"Excuse me, M'Lord, but Willy'd like to speak to Your Lordship."

'Willy?" the Marquis asked, not recognising the name.

"He's the knife-boy, M'Lord," Dalton explained, "whose finger Miss Ula treated when he cut himself."

"You say he wants to see me?" the Marquis asked.

"It seems impertinent of him, M'Lord, but he says he's something to tell Your Lordship about Miss Ula, and he refuses to divulge to me what it is."

There was a note of irritation in Dalton's voice which the Marquis did not miss.

He rose from the chair in which he was sitting and said:

"Send Willy into the Library."

As he left the Drawing-Room there was an expression of hope in the Duchess's eyes, but he thought the knife-boy was probably making things worse than they already were.

It was unlikely that he could contribute anything useful to all their interminable discussions about Ula's whereabouts.

He had not waited for more than a minute when there was a tentative knock on the door and Willy came in.

He was a thin boy of about fifteen and he looked intelligent, although he was obviously shy and very overawed by his master.

"You wished to see me, Willy?" the Marquis asked in a quiet tone.

He sat down as he spoke, thinking the boy would find him less overpowering than when he was standing.

Willy twisted his fingers together, then almost as if the words burst from him he said:

" 'T'is about Miss Ula, M'Lord."

"If you think you can tell me something which will help me find her,' the Marquis said, "I shall of course be very grateful."

" 'Er were very kind t'me, M'Lord."

"I know that. Tell me anything you think might help me in my search to find her."

The Marquis spoke in the same tone of voice he had used in the Army which had made a young recruit find it easy to confide in him.

Willy took a deep breath.

" 'T'is loik this, M'Lord, when Oi tells Miss Ula Oi were an orphan, 'er said 'er were one too, an' misses 'er Pa and Ma jus' loik Oi misses moin."

Willy seemed to take a gulp of air as if he had spoken without breathing and the Marquis said:

"Take your time, I am listening, and I am very interested."

"Miss Ula says to Oi, M'Lord, that even if we can't see 'em, they're allus lookin' a'ter us, an' still lovin' us. An' Oi

131

says to 'er, Oi says: "T'is 'ard ter believe that when Oi'm all alone.'

"An' 'er says to Oi, 'er says:

" 'When I go ter bed at night I pretend Oi'm still at 'ome in the 'ouse where I was so 'appy when my father and mother were near me, loving me, and Oi'm safe as they're there.' "

Willy paused again. He knew the Marquis was listening and after a moment he went on:

"Then 'er says to me, 'er says, 'I loves my 'ome an' one day I shall go back an' although my father and mother'll not be there, I shall feel their love be still lingering on th' walls and tho' 't'is very small, to me 't'is more wonderful thar any other house could be.' "

Willy's voice softened as he said:

"There were tears in me eyes, M'Lord, when 'er said that, and Oi thinks that if 'er were un'appy or frightened, that's where 'er 'ud go – 'ome!"

The Marquis looked at the knife-boy in astonishment, then he said:

"Of course she would! It was very clever of you, Willy, to think of it and to be brave enough to tell me so. I will go to Worcestershire where I know she lived and, if I find her, I shall certainly reward you for helping me."

"Oi wants no reward, M'Lord," Willy said, "Oi jus' want ter know Miss Ula's not dead, as they says 'er be. 'Er more kind t'me than anybody's ever bin since me Ma died."

His voice broke and as if he did not wish the Marquis to see him crying he put his knuckles in his eyes and went away from the room.

The Marquis rose to his feet with an expression on his face that would have surprised his grandmother.

Ula, travelling with the Gypsies, found the days seemed to stretch out.

It was difficult to know how long the wheels of the caravans had been moving beneath her, and how many

132

nights she had sat around the camp-fire in some quiet wood or in the corner of an uncultivated field.

She slept in a caravan with Zokka and her small sister, the two girls sleeping in one bed, while Ula had the other.

Like all caravans, which to the Gypsies were sacred, it was spotlessly clean inside and so were the clothes, although a little worn, that Zokka had lent her.

They were of about the same size, and although Ula was not aware of it, she looked very attractive in the full short red skirt and the white blouse with a velvet corselet which encircled her small waist and laced up down the front.

Because she was fair, despite the fact that she always hid in the caravan if they passed through a village, Ula covered her hair with a coloured handkerchief.

There was little she could do about her fair skin and the blue of her eyes.

She was far too frightened however of being discovered by her Uncle not to be prepared at any moment of the day to creep inside the caravan if ever a carriage and horses came into sight.

She was frightened too that her Uncle might hire the Bow Street Runners to help in his search for her.

She also had the terrifying feeling that in fact her Uncle might be less persistent in his pursuit of her than Prince Hasin.

But while the thought of him terrified her in the daytime, and she started at the sound of an unknown voice, at night she thought only of the Marquis.

When the only sound in the caravan was of the two girls' soft breathing, she would lie awake thinking of his handsome face.

She knew, whatever happened to her, she would love him for the rest of her life.

She loved everything about him, his laughter, his keen perception and witty brain, his square shoulders and strong hands.

Even though she knew they were an affectation, she

loved even his drooping eyelids and drawling voice.

"I love him . . I love him!" she murmured into her pillow.

She wondered if he ever thought of her now that she had disappeared.

Or was he too busy with the lovely Georgina Cavendish or any other of the beauties who would be eagerly waiting for his attention?

Sometimes she would dream that he was holding her in his arms and she need no longer be afraid either of her Uncle or of Prince Hasin.

Then she remembered her Uncle's threats that he would accuse the Marquis of abducting a minor.

Even if the Earl could not prove the Marquis to be guilty, it would cause a scandal and the Marquis would loathe the publicity that such an assertion would evoke.

What it meant, Ula argued to herself, was that she must not only avoid her Uncle and Prince Hasin, but also the Marquis whom she loved.

If she was found in his presence it might do him harm.

Then because she could not help herself, the tears would run down her cheeks, for if she could never see the Marquis again, the world seemed an unutterably dark and empty place without sunshine.

When morning came she told herself she had to be brave and make plans for the future, even if she was a fugitive.

She wondered if, when she arrived back at the little village where she had lived all her life, somebody would be kind enough to let her stay with them until she could find work and be able to keep herself.

She was sure old Graves and his wife whom her father had pensioned off just before he was killed would help her.

They were a dear old couple, and Graves had gone on working in the garden even after he had retired.

Mrs Graves, however, was too rheumaticky and old to scrub the kitchen any longer or climb the stairs to help with the beds.

'They loved Papa and Mama,' Ula thought. 'I know they would help me, but I must earn some money quickly, for they could not afford to feed me out of their tiny pension.'

It was, however, a comforting thought to know that, like the Graveses, many people in the Parish had loved both her father and mother.

They would, she was certain, wish to save her from having to marry a man like Prince Hasin.

At the same time, she was aware that she would have to be very, very careful that they were not involved in such a way that her Uncle could make them suffer for their kindness to her.

In the meantime she was extremely grateful to the Gypsies.

In order to pay her way she helped the women make wicker baskets in which they could put the clothes pegs they sold from door to door in the villages.

Being able to sew well, Ula also made a number of colourful little bags from the rags the Gypsies accumulated while they were passing through the countryside.

The girls said that they would fill them with pot-pourri or lavender as soon as they had the opportunity.

Because Ula was a blood sister of the Gypsies they treated her as one of themselves, and were not shy or tongue-tied as they were usually with strangers.

They told her their troubles and she also learnt some of their magic spells.

When Zokka and her sister crept away from the camp-fire when the moon was full to send out a wish that they might have a handsome lover, Ula went with them.

Even though she knew such a wish was hopeless, she could not help thinking of the Marquis and praying that by some miracle he would love her a little.

"Just a little . . a very little . . " she whispered, looking up into the brilliance of the full moon.

But when she returned to where the rest of the Gypsies were sitting, she told herself she was asking the impossible and the Marquis was as far out of reach as the moon itself.

Ula could never remember afterwards how long it was before they reached the county in which she had been born.

Something within her responded immediately to the rows of fruit trees and the undulating countryside with the River Avon silver as a moonbeam moving through it.

The Gypsies assured her it was no trouble to take her to the small village where she had lived with her father and mother.

"It's on our way," they said, "and we'll wait until we're certain you have somebody to stay with before we leave. If there is no one, you'll come with us."

"You have been so kind to me already," Ula said, "I must not impose on you any further."

"You're not imposing," the Gypsies said simply, "for as your blood's our blood you belong to us."

"Of course you do!" Zokka said, and kissed her.

The Gypsies drew into the small field where the Gypsies Ula had known as a child had always camped.

She hoped that by some marvellous coincidence they might be there.

But she knew it was too early in the season for them as they had always come later in the year.

There were still faint marks where the fires had singed the grass, and the caravans rested in the shelter of the trees before Ula alighted.

Moving a little way along the side of the road she saw the gabled black and white house which had been her home for seventeen years.

For a moment she could only see it through her tears. Then as she went a little nearer she was aware that it seemed to be uninhabited.

She had expected that as soon as she had left and her Uncle had sold everything her father and mother had possessed to pay their debts, another incumbent would have been appointed in her father's place.

Looking at the house now it was obvious that the

windows were all closed and uncurtained, while the garden was a riot of flowers with a wildness that had never been there before.

'It seems strange,' Ula thought.

Then with a sudden lift of her spirits an idea came to her that she might be able to hide in the house.

She moved nearer and nearer, creeping along the side of the hedge which bordered the garden.

Then when she came to the gate which led into it she saw working in the distance a bent figure she recognised as old Graves.

He was there in the back garden which was kept for the growing of vegetables.

Because she was so pleased to see him, Ula opened the gate and ran along the path that was badly in need of weeding, through the lilac and syringa bushes, and on until she reached him.

He was little changed except that he had less hair than she remembered and what was left of it was dead white.

As he saw her he straightened up and said wonderingly:

"Be that ye, Miss Ula?"

She pulled the handkerchief off her head.

"Yes, Graves. Do not say you have forgotten me!"

" 'Course not," he said stoutly, "but Oi 'ears as 'ow ye were lost."

"How did you hear that?" Ula asked quickly.

"Two men come 'ere askin' for ye. Grooms, oi thinks they was."

"Are they still here?" Ula asked in a frightened voice.

Graves shook his head.

"Nah, they be gone – three days since, and when Oi says Oi ain't seen a sign o' ye, they goes back where they comes from."

Ula thought they were very likely her Uncle's grooms, and she said with a little sigh:

"Nobody must know that I am here. Who is living in the house?"

"Ain't no one," Graves replied. "New Vicar said 't'were too small for 'e, an' moved into t'old Manor next t'Church. Ye remembers it, Miss Ula?"

"Yes, of course," Ula agreed.

The Manor House was certainly bigger and very much more impressive than the little Vicarage which had been quite large enough for her father and mother.

From where she was standing she could see the ancient grey Church in which she had been christened and it gave her a feeling of security almost as if her father was beside her.

"If there is nobody living in the house, Graves, I would like to go inside."

'Oi've got t'key, Miss Ula, as I keeps me tools in there."

She looked at him for explanation and he went on:

"Bishop say Oi gotta be caretaker of t'old Vicarage, as they now calls it, in case they moight want it agin. Oi grows a few vegetables in the garden, bu' Oi can't do as much as I used to do."

"No, of course not," Ula said sympathetically, "but I would like to go into the house."

The old man fumbled in his pocket until he found the key which he gave to Ula.

"I will look around," she said, "and then I want to talk to you."

"Oi'll be 'ere, Miss Ula, don' ye worry. Ye'll find some o' the things they couldn't sell upstairs in t'attic. Oi 'ad 'em put there for safety."

Ula gave him a smile, then because she could not wait she hurried towards the back-door and opening it walked into her home.

Almost instantly she felt as if her mother and father were beside her and she need no longer be afraid.

The rooms on the ground floor were all empty, except for a few pieces of carpet that had not been worth selling and an occasional curtain that had been too tatty to fetch even a penny or two.

Ula however was seeing the rooms as she had last seen them.

Her mother was doing the flowers in the vases in the Sitting-Room, while her father was writing his sermons at a desk in the room next door.

Then she went up the stairs.

Although the big bed and the white furniture which had graced her mother's bedroom had gone, she felt as if the walls vibrated with the love that had existed between two people who had adored each other.

She felt the same in her own small room which was next door, and which had always seemed to her to be filled with light and laughter.

"I have come home," she said aloud as she walked down the passage and up the small twisting staircase which led to the attic.

As Graves had said, everything which had not been saleable had been put upstairs.

There were cracked bowls and china ewers from the bedrooms, there were saucepans and pans from the kitchen.

Hanging on the wall were several gowns of hers and her mother's which must have been too small for anyone in the village.

Or perhaps where her mother was concerned, they were superstitious about wearing the clothes of a dead woman.

'At least I have something to wear,' Ula thought.

At the same time she could see the gowns were in fact not very suitable for somebody who had to earn their living by working in the fields!

This was the most likely job to be found in the neighbourhood, or else scrubbing floors.

But she did not worry about that now while there were other memories to be found.

Books from her father's Study, mostly religious treatises, and what she felt was very precious, the Bible he had always used personally.

She was holding it in her hand and looking down at his name inscribed in his firm handwriting, when she heard somebody moving about downstairs.

Instantly, like an animal that is being hunted, she was alert and tense, standing very still, listening.

There were footsteps, moving too swiftly for it to be Graves.

Then she thought that the old man must have been mistaken.

The men who had come in search of her several days ago had been clever enough to reason that sooner or later she would turn up.

They had waited for just this moment, and she felt a sense of panic sweep over her.

She looked around and saw that the only possible place for her to hide was behind some packing-cases which were standing in the centre of the attic.

They were doubtless filled with more broken china and unusable utensils like those that were scattered on the floor.

Swiftly as a fox hiding from those who were hunting it, she ran to the crates and crouched down behind them.

She was hoping that anyone who stood just inside the door would not see her.

Even as she made herself as small as possible she heard the footsteps coming up the stairs.

The door of the attic was open and as the man reached it, Ula's heart was beating so frantically that she felt it must jump from her breast.

She was praying desperately for her father's protection.

"Save me .. Papa .. save me .. you led me to the Gypsies and I am here .. do not let them .. catch me now .. please Papa .. please .. !"

She was praying with every nerve in her body strained with the anxiety of her fear.

At the same time, she was acutely conscious that the man who had followed her was standing just inside the doorway and she was sure was looking for her.

Then softly a voice asked:

"Are you there, Ula?"

For a moment she thought she must be dreaming and could not have heard correctly.

Then with a little cry she rose from where she was hiding and saw standing amongst the debris the elegant figure of the Marquis.

For a moment they just stared at each other. Then Ula felt that he held out his arms and without thinking she ran towards him.

She flung herself against him, his arms went around her, and his lips were on hers, holding her captive.

He kissed her wildly, passionately, possessively, drawing her closer and closer.

It was as if it was the only way in which he could express what he was feeling, and there were no words in which he could do so.

To Ula it was as if the skies had opened and she had been swept from the very depths of despair and fear into a blinding light.

It was so glorious, so utterly and completely wonderful, that it could only be part of the Divine.

Then as the Marquis kissed her and went on kissing her, she thought because it could not be true that she must have died.

Only when they were both breathless and Ula could feel his heart beating frantically against hers did the Marquis raise his head and say in a curiously unsteady voice:

"I have found you! Where have you been? I have been frantic with worry!"

He thought as he looked down at Ula that he had never thought it possible for a woman to look so beautiful and at the same so utterly and completely radiant.

He thought too that with her fair hair falling like a child's on to her shoulders, she looked even more like an angel than he remembered.

"You have . . found me," Ula said, "and I . . thought I should . . never see you . . again!"

There was a lilt in the way she spoke and her voice held a rapture which made the Marquis without replying merely kiss her.

Now as he was aware of the softness, sweetness and innocence of her lips, he was more gentle, at the same time very demanding, almost as if he took possession of her.

When at last she could speak Ula asked in a hesitating, yet lilting voice:

"Why . . are you here . . and why . . are you . . looking at me?"

"Could you expect me to do anything else?" the Marquis asked. "It was clever of you, my darling, but you must have known that I would save you."

"I . . I thought even if you wanted to . . you would not be . . in time," Ula said, "and . . I would rather . . have died than marry Prince Hasin."

"And I would have killed him before I would let him become your husband!" the Marquis said.

The way he spoke made her look at him in astonishment. Then she said:

"I thought . . perhaps when I had gone . . you . . might have been . . glad to be . . rid of me."

The Marquis's arms tightened about her.

"How could you think anything so absurd?" he asked. "And how could you do anything so cruel as to leave everybody in tears, especially my grandmother and Willy?"

Ula looked at him as if she could hardly believe what he was saying, and he went on:

"I was frantic, absolutely frantic when no one could find you!"

"But . . you looked?"

"Of course I looked!" he replied. "I searched the whole countryside: the woods, the fields, the villages, all day, every day, until Willy told me what I should have thought of myself, that you would have come home."

"Willy . . told you?"

"It was something you said to him about pretending at night to be back in your home and how one day you would come back."

"So you found me."

The words were redolent with relief. Then she gave a little cry of fear.

"Uncle Lionel! He has already . . sent men here to . . look for me, and perhaps they will . . come again. You must hide me . . please . . you do not . . understand . . he has the . . law on his . . side."

"I know that," the Marquis said, "and that is why I intend to hide you so effectively that never again can he threaten you or make you afraid."

Instinctively, Ula moved a little closer to him as she said:

"It sounds . . wonderful . . but how can . . you do . . that?"

"Easily," the Marquis replied very quietly. "We are going to be married!"

For a moment Ula felt that she could not have heard him aright.

Then she stared at him, thinking she had never seen him look so happy or so young, and he said:

"Everything is arranged. I have just been waiting for you."

"I . . I do not . . understand."

"Tell me first," he said, "how you got here without money, and wearing when you left Chessington Hall only your nightgown?"

Ula smiled at him, then she moved from his arms so that she was not so close to him.

"Look at me."

The Marquis's eyes were on her face.

"I am looking," he said. "I had almost forgotten how lovely you are; so sweet, so perfect, so untouched! My precious, how can I tell you how much I love you and how different you are from any other woman I have ever known?"

"Are you . . really saying . . such things to . . me?" Ula asked in a whisper.

"I have a great deal more to say," the Marquis answered, "but time is passing, and we cannot stand here for the rest of our lives."

It suddenly struck Ula how funny it was.

The Marquis of Raventhorpe, who owned so many houses filled with treasures, standing and declaring himself in a low-ceilinged attic surrounded by broken chairs and china and old saucepans that were too dilapidated to be sold.

Then as she looked into his eyes she knew that any place where she was with the Marquis would seem like a Temple of Beauty.

Because she loved him so overwhelmingly, this place was sacred.

"I love . . you," she whispered, and saw the expression in the Marquis's eyes which told her without words how much he loved her.

"I want to kiss you," he said, "and nothing else is really important, but we have a great deal to do and you have not answered my question."

"You have not looked at my dress."

He glanced down at her, at the velvet corselet around her waist, the white blouse and the full red skirt.

"The Gypsies!" he exclaimed. "You have been with the Gypsies!"

"They brought me here and they are camping in the field where Gypsies have always camped ever since I was a child."

"And you were safe with them? They did not harm you?"

"No, of course not!" Ula smiled. "Anyway, I am their blood sister."

"One day you must tell me all about it," the Marquis

144

answered, "but now the Vicar who has taken your father's place will be waiting for us."

He kissed her on the forehead before he said:

"Once you are my wife, my darling, no one shall hurt or insult you, and if any man tries to take you from me, I will kill him!"

For a moment Ula could only look at him and her eyes seemed to fill her whole face. Then she said almost inarticulately:

"It . . it cannot be . . true . . that you really . . want to . . m . marry me!"

"I intend to marry you!" the Marquis said firmly. "There is no other way I can make sure that you never leave me, and never make me so unhappy, so frightened, and so frantic as I have been these last ten days."

"Is is really ten days since I ran away?" Ula asked.

"It seems to me like ten centuries," the Marquis said, "but I knew after what Willy told me that you would eventually come here, and that is why I have been waiting."

He smiled and Ula thought the lines of his cynicism had disappeared, and there was a boyish note in his voice as he said:

"Come on! Hurry! And while we have been talking here you will find a gown for you to wear waiting for you downstairs."

"A . . a gown?" Ula questioned.

By this time the Marquis was going down the narrow stairway to the first floor and drawing her after him by the hand.

As they reached the passage he said:

"I could hardly expect to marry you in your nightgown, adorable though I am sure you look in it. So I have brought a trunkful of clothes with me, and when we have time we will buy your trousseau."

"I am dreaming . . I know I am . . dreaming!" Ula said.

The Marquis did not answer.

He only drew her into what had been her mother's bedroom where, in the middle of it on a small square of carpet which had not been sold, stood a leather trunk.

Somebody had opened it and on top lay a white gown which she knew without picking it up had been designed for a bride.

Beside it was a wreath of orange blossom resting on a veil.

"How can you have . . thought of it?" Ula asked. "And also have been so . . certain you would . . find me . . here?"

The Marquis thought for a moment of the agony he had suffered when he had sent the divers to search the river.

But everything would keep until they had time to talk.

All he wanted now was that Ula should become his wife, so that it would be impossible for her to be spirited away from him by her uncle or anyone else.

He was, although he did not say so to Ula, still afraid that Prince Hasin who, like many Eastern potentates, would use any unscrupulous means to obtain his desires, would still be pursuing her.

He already knew that besides the Earl's servants who were searching there were some dark, rather sinister men who were employed by the Prince.

He therefore asked:

"Can you manage to dress yourself?"

"Of course," Ula dimpled, "it is something I have always done."

"Then hurry," the Marquis said. "When I saw you coming to the house, I sent one of my grooms to tell the Vicar to be waiting for us in the Church and I do not wish him to become impatient."

Ula laughed.

Then as the Marquis left her alone she pulled off her Gypsy clothing and put on the white gown which was even more beautiful than the gowns the Duchess had bought for her.

It was a wedding-gown that any girl would gladly dream of possessing.

Fortunately in one of the cupboards of her mother's room there was a mirror attached to the back of the door.

Standing in front of it she was able to arrange her hair with the few hairpins she had left, and to cover it with the veil and the orange blossom wreath.

Then feeling excited, as if the whole world had turned topsy-turvy, but was amazing in a manner that defied expression, she opened the door and started down the stairs.

The Marquis was waiting for her in the hall, and as she looked at him she knew he was the most handsome and attractive man she had ever seen.

There was also now vibrating from him everything she had wanted from him but which in the past she had missed.

She knew they were the vibrations that came not only from his mind but from his heart.

Because he was in love everything that had belittled his grandeur and his nobility had disappeared.

Now he was exactly as she wanted him to be.

He was a man who would do great things not only for her, but for other people, because, as her father would have said, a Divine Power was flowing through him.

At the moment, although all she wanted to do was to tell him of her love, as his eyes met hers she knew there was no need for words.

They were already so close and belonged to each other so completely that even the Sacrament of marriage could not make them any closer than they already were.

Holding her hand, the Marquis drew her through the front-door and outside where she saw his Phaeton was waiting.

He picked her up in his arms and lifted her into it.

As the grooms climbed up behind Ula saw there were two outriders riding ahead of them to lead them the short distance to the Church.

She thought they were there not only for protection on the roads just in case they should be held up by highwaymen.

They were also there so that neither the Earl nor the Prince, nor anyone else, could stop the Marquis from marrying her.

There were only a few old villagers to look at them in surprise as they drove up to the porch of the West Door.

The Marquis put down the reins and rounding the Phaeton took her in his arms to lift her down.

"I love you!" he said in his deep voice. "And when we are married I will be able to tell you how much."

She slipped her arm through his, and as they entered the Church where she had worshipped all her life she could hear the organ playing softly.

She felt that both her father and her mother were very close to her and she could feel their presence as she and the Marquis were joined together by the beautiful words of the Marriage Service.

When he put the ring on her finger she felt as if there were angel voices singing a paean of praise, while the Church was filled not with people, but with love.

Then as they knelt and received the blessing, Ula told herself that no one could be more lucky than she had been.

Not only in finding the man she loved, but in knowing that he loved her as her father and mother had loved each other.

"Thank You . . oh, thank You . . God!" she said in her heart.

She vowed that her whole life would in future be an expression of gratitude for what she had received.

They walked down the aisle and the Marquis once again lifted her into his Phaeton and drove off, but not returning, as she had expected they would, to her home.

"Where are we going?" she asked.

Because she could not help it she moved a little closer to him so that she could lay her hand on his knee.

He looked down at her with a smile.

She knew he was feeling as she was that they were dedicated in their gratitude because they were together, and now no one could separate them.

"We are going to spend the night in a house I have been loaned by the Lord Lieutenant, who is a friend of mine," the Marquis replied. "No one can possibly find us there, and there will be no disruptions."

He smiled as he went on:

"Then tomorrow we are going to my home in Oxfordshire, which will be yours, my precious, in the future. After that, we are setting out on our honeymoon which will be a surprise."

"It sounds . . too perfect," Ula murmured.

Then she gave a little cry.

"The Gypsies! I must let them know what has happened to me."

"I thought of that, and while you were dressing I sent one of my grooms to tell them you were to be married, and also to express your gratitude and mine for their kindness in a more practical manner."

"I hope they will not be insulted that you gave them money," Ula said quickly.

"I told my groom to be very tactful," the Marquis replied, "and I also informed them that any Gypsies in the future would always be welcome on any estate I own."

"You could not have given them a better present!" Ula exclaimed.

They drove on and came to the house where the Marquis had been staying while he waited for her.

It was very pretty, beautifully appointed, and she learned later that the Lord Lieutenant had been preparing it for one of his relatives who had been abroad for some time.

Everything about it was fresh and bright and, Ula thought, very beautiful as well as a perfect background for the occasion.

There were discreet servants to wait on them, and when they had finished luncheon the Marquis took her upstairs.

They went into a beautifully decorated bedroom with a large bed draped with silk curtains which were as blue as her eyes, falling from a carved gold corolla.

"What a lovely room!" she exclaimed.

"I thought, my darling," the Marquis said, "you would want to change from your wedding-gown, and your trunk which was brought here while we were having luncheon has been unpacked."

She smiled at him.

"You think of everything!"

"I think of you," he answered. "How can I think of anything else when you are so perfect and exactly what I always wanted my wife to be."

Just for a moment Ula thought of Sarah.

As if the Marquis read her thoughts he said:

"Forget about her! We all make mistakes in our lives, and from now on your job, my lovely one, is to see that I make as few as possible in the future."

As he spoke he lifted her wreath from her head, then her veil, and taking out the pins which held her hair in place let it fall over her shoulders.

"Now you look like the angel you are," he said, "my angel, who will guide and inspire me for the rest of my life."

"Can I . . really do . . that?" Ula asked.

"It is what you have done already," the Marquis replied, "and because of you I am very different from the man I was before."

"I love you . . just as you . . are," she whispered.

Because she could not help it, she moved closer to him. Then as he kissed her she felt him undoing her wedding-gown.

As it fell to the ground with the softness of a sigh he picked her up in his arms and carried her to the canopied bed.

She lay against the soft pillows feeling as if she was

floating on a cloud and that once again she was dreaming.

Then as the Marquis joined her she knew it was no dream but a glorious reality, so that once again her whole being was lifted up in a prayer of gratitude.

But as she felt the Marquis's lips on hers, his hand touching her, his body hard against the softness of hers, she could think of nothing but him.

"I . . love you . . I love . . you!" she whispered.

"I worship you," he replied, "and it is something I shall do, my beloved, all my life!"

As she spoke he felt her quiver from the movements of his hand to a first awakening to sensuousness, and thought it the most exciting thing he had ever known.

"You are not frightened?" he asked.

"A . . little!"

"I will be very gentle."

"I am not . . frightened . . of you."

"Then of what, my precious?"

"Perhaps you will . . find me . . dull and . . disappointing and you . . will no longer . . love me . . and I will be all . . alone again!"

"My Angel, that is impossible!"

"Why?"

"Because I do not only love you for your beauty and for your exquisite body, but I adore your kind heart and more than anything else what is called your 'soul' which will make me love and worship you for ever."

"How can you say such wonderful . . wonderful . . things to me?"

The tears ran down Ula's cheeks as she asked:

"Do you really think . . I have the . . Divine Light which Papa said was . . so important?"

"To me," the Marquis answered, "you shine like a star in the darkness – a star which I will follow all my life."

"Oh, darling . . darling . . I love . . you."

He kissed the tears away from Ula's cheeks.

Then as he held her closer still, she felt as if there were

shafts of light flowing from his body into hers and from his mind into her mind.

She knew it was the Power of Divine Love which was not, as she had thought, soft and gentle as the moonlight, but burning, as the heat of the sun.

She could feel it sweeping through her and rising from her breasts into her lips to meet the fire within the Marquis.

She knew then that love was strong, overpowering and an irresistible force that would drive them into doing great deeds and seeking far horizons.

The ecstasy and glory of it was a rapture beyond words.

The Marquis made her his and they became one, not only with their bodies but with their minds and their hearts.

The Divine Power carried them into the Heaven that exists for all those who find the true love which comes from God.

It is the beauty and perfection of Eternal Life.

OTHER BOOKS BY BARBARA CARTLAND

Romantic Novels, over 395, the most recently published being

The Scots Never Forget
The Rebel Princess
A Witch's Spell
Secrets
The Storms of Love
Moonlight on the Sphinx
White Lilac
Revenge of the Heart
Bride to a Brigand
Love Comes West
The Island of Love
Theresa and a Tiger
Love is Heaven
Miracle for a Madonna
A Very Unusual Wife
The Peril and the Prince
Alone and Afraid
Terror for a Teacher
The Devilish Deception
In Paradise
The Dream and the Glory (in aid of the St John Ambulance Brigade)

Autobiographical and Biographical
The Isthmus Years 1919-1939
The Years of Opportunity 1939-1945
I Search for Rainbows 1945-1976
We Danced All Night 1919-1929
Ronald Cartland (with a Foreword by Sir Winston Churchill)
Polly My Wonderful Mother
I Seek the Miraculous

Historical:
Bewitching Women
The Outrageous Queen (The story of Queen Christina of Sweden)
The Scandalous Life of King Carol
The Private Life of Elizabeth, Empress of Austria
Josephine, Empress of France
Diane de Poitiers
Metternich – the Passionate Diplomat
The Private Life of Charles II

Sociology:
You in the Home
The Fascinating Forties
Marriage for Moderns
Be Vivid, Be Vital
Love, Life and Sex
Vitamins for Vitality
Husbands and Wives
Men are Wonderful
Etiquette
The Many Facets of Love
Sex and the Teenager
The Book of Charm
Living Together
The Youth Secret
The Magic of Honey
Book of Beauty and Health
Keep Young and Beautiful by Barbara Cartland and Elinor Glynn
Book of Health

Cookery:
Barbara Cartland's Health Food and Cookery Book
Food for Love
Magic of Honey Cookbook

Recipes for Lovers
The Romance of Food

Editor of:
The Common Problem by Ronald Cartland (with a preface by the
Rt. Hon. the Earl of Selborne, P.C.)
Barbara Cartland's Library of Love
Barbara Cartland's Library of Ancient Wisdom

Written with Love
Passionate love letters selected by Barbara Cartland

Drama:
Blood Money
French Dressing

Philosophy:
Touch the Stars

Radio Operetta:
The Rose and the Violet (Music by Mark Lubbock) performed in
1942.

Radio Plays:
The Caged Bird: An episode in the Life of Elizabeth Empress of
Austria. Performed in 1957.

General:
Barbara Cartland's Book of Useless Information, with a Fore-
word by The Earl Mountbatten of Burma. (In aid of the United
World Colleges)
Love and Lovers Picture Book
The Light of Love (Prayer Book)
Barbara Cartland's Scrapbook (in Aid of the Royal Photographic
Museum)
Romantic Royal Marriages
Barbara Cartland's Book of Celebrities

Getting Older, Growing Younger

Verse:
Lines on Life and Love

Music:
An Album of Love Songs sung with the Royal Philharmonic Orchestra.

Film:
The Flame is Love

Cartoons:
Barbara Cartland Romances (Book of Cartoons) has recently been published in the U.S.A. and Great Britain and in other parts of the world. Getting Older, Growing Younger and The Romance of Food were also published in these countries.

Children's Pop-Up Book:
Princess to the Rescue.

Barbara Cartland
Love is a Gamble £1.75

Idona was horrified to learn that before her father was killed in a duel he had gambled away his house, his estate, and even herself to the Marquis of Wroxham. Her first unconventional meeting with this cynical dandy led to his introducing Idona to London society as his ward. Idona soon fled back to the country, bewildered by the intrigues and deceptions. Only when the Marquis followed did she realise that the turn of a card had won them the most precious prize in the world – love.

Alone and Afraid £1.75

On holiday in Paris, the Marquis of Elkesley found himself unexpectedly guardian to Kitrina, the obviously illegitimate daughter of his cousin who had run away with one of Queen Victoria's ladies-in-waiting. Even as he strove to foil the evil plans of Sheik Hassan who coveted Kitrina's blonde lovelines for his harem, the Marquis realised that it was hopeless to fight against the love he felt. But how could he take Kitrina home to face the contempt and condemnation society afforded to a girl born out of wedlock?

Temptation for a Teacher £1.75

Faced with the necessity of earning her own living Lady Arletta Cherrington-Weir gladly impersonated a friend and went as a governess to the Dordogne. An atmosphere of menace and mystery surrounded the beautiful castle of Etienne, Duc de Sauterre. Known to have an obsessive hatred of things English, he was feared by everyone and even suspected of murder. Innocent victim of a wicked conspiracy, Arletta little thought that by falling in love with Etienne she was condemning them both to a watery grave.

Barbara Cartland
A Victory for Love £1.75

Farica had gone riding to try and decide whether to please her father and marry the new Earl of Lydbrooke while knowing that he was only interested in her fortune. A chance meeting with John Hamilton, badly wounded at Waterloo, was to make up her mind . . .

A Very Unusual Wife £1.50

The reputation of the Marquis of Falcon was such that Queen Victoria would bestow no further honour on him until he was married. His offer for the youngest daughter of the Earl of Warnborough brought him many surprises, not least Elmina's use of karate to repel his unwanted advances on their wedding night. Only when Elmina's life is in danger does the Marquis realise his love for her, and rides like a whirlwind to answer her silent prayers.

Safe at Last £1.75

Otila Ashe was a wealthy young heiress, a tempting prize, and a man-hater. Desperate to escape from Paris and a menacing future she turned in her hour of need to Lord Kirkly, a confessed woman-hater. Pursued across the frontier into Italy by a vindictive fortune-seeking French family they needed all their ingenuity to keep ahead. As her would—be captors closed in, Otila and Lord Kirkly found their answer in a love so compelling that they could only surrender to its divine power.